Miranda's meetings with Shakespeare

William Shakespeare statue in Leicester Square, London

Miranda's meetings with Shakespeare

Bryan Ritz

A Backstage Book

First published in Great Britain by Backstage Books 2012

ISBN 978-0-9544727-1-9

Photographic illustrations by Talia Lehavi, Viv Mullett and Bryan Ritz
*Edited for publication by Carolyn Manley, former Head of Drama,
Queens College, London, and Janet Donovan*
Designed, typeset and produced by The Flying Fish Studios Ltd

Printed by Gomer Press, Llandysul, Wales

Backstage Books information and for sales and enquiries:
Website: www.backstagebooks.co.uk
E-mail: info@backstagebooks.co.uk
Telephone: (+0044) (0)1923 248294
*All Backstage Books can be purchased through our website
or through www.amazon.co.uk*

Backstage Books
www.backstagebooks.co.uk

*The story is published
in fond memory of Ronald and Irene Ritz*

Costumes for photographs courtesy of
The Royal National Theatre
Costume and Furniture Hire Department,
1-3 Brixton Road, London SW9 6DE

Props for photographs courtesy of
Triumph Entertainment's
production of The Tempest *at*
The Old Vic Theatre
The Cut, Waterloo, London SE1 8NB

Grateful thanks to Picton Castle, Pembrokeshire, Wales
for allowing access to photograph the spiral staircase
and Tudor portrait

All play quotations from The Arden Shakespeare editions

Tarot drawings based on images by Lo Scarabeo, Torino, Italy

Playhouse illustration based on drawings by J.H. Farrar,
New York University Press

Special thanks to:
Carolyn Manley and Janet Donovan
Support and advice: Nicola Ritz, Sheila Harrison and Carl Lynch
Cover and frontispiece photographs: Zoran Matic
Thanks to: Gabrielle Reffell, Agatha Doorley and Nadine Itani

With special recognition of lectures and writings by
Raymond Armin

Contents

Introduction

The year is 1611. Within the walls of the ancient monastery of Blackfriars, situated at the edge of the City of London, the King's Men acting troupe have created a unique indoor Playhouse where a fantastical world is played out for their audiences, in an age where there was no TV, cinema or Internet. They summon royalty, emperors and rulers long passed away to exercise their power again and act out their intrigues on stage. Fourteen-year-old Miranda observes by chance a rehearsal for the production of their most ground-breaking and mystical play *The Tempest*, written by their principal playwright William Shakespeare. This begins a series of exciting adventures and with the help of the boy players she befriends, she discovers some of the secrets of the Playhouse and pursues her own desire to act on the stage. She discovers some of the philosophical inspiration for the playwright's work and Sir Francis Bacon's special contribution to the plays.

Suitable for readers aged eleven and over, this story will help the development of literacy, as well as bringing Jacobean theatre history to life.

The first part of these tales has been adapted from *A Play for Miranda*, first published in 2003 by Bryan Ritz.

Part One

Early Spring 1611

A Secret Meeting

A flash of lightning lit up the deep indigo sky as a teenage girl wearing a long cloak ran across the cobblestones in search of shelter at the side of an ancient monastery. The swirling dark clouds opened and hail stones teemed down, crashing and bouncing on the moss-covered gravestones in a small disused cemetery. Desperate to find refuge from the torrent of rain that followed she edged her way into a recess under a covered cloister, once housing a statue of a saint. Miranda's long auburn hair was now wet as she pulled up her collar to keep warm and waited for the thunderstorm to pass.

While watching the heavy downpour cascading from the steep roof of the Gate-House along the lane, she recalled her first visit here with her wonderfully wise and learned uncle. Peter was a retired apothecary and had brought her to the monastery to see a performance of William Shakespeare's *The Winter's Tale* for her fourteenth birthday and she had been deeply impressed

The apothecary at Blackfriars

by the whole experience of seeing the play. He was very supportive of Miranda's education and encouraged her to ask him as many questions as she wanted about the place and the mysterious acting troupe who used the grand meeting chamber as their theatre.

He told her that within the ancient monastery hidden like a jewel, the Blackfriars Playhouse was the most discussed phenomenon in the City. The *King's Men* troupe were said to be able to summon royalty, emperors and rulers long passed away to exercise their power again and act out their intrigues on stage. Through special arts, known only to a select few, they were renowned for inviting the famous and the infamous from history to walk again on earth through their plays. But that was not all. They were respected as masters of comedy, romantic drama, magical fantasy and their boy players represented the epitome and apotheosis of female portrayal in an age when women could not act on the stage. Their most famous playwright William Shakespeare had earned notability at Court and a considerable fortune. There was even talk that hidden knowledge had been encrypted into the texts, making the plays some of the most philosophically inspired productions ever performed in the Western world.

Miranda's first impression when she came here was that the monastery was a little eerie and there was talk of ghosts that roamed the corridors and halls. However once inside the grand chamber that had been converted into the most awe-inspiring theatre she had ever seen, she felt it was more like a cathedral than a playhouse. Despite the lofty height of the tiered rows of seats and the wide stage, with two smaller stages above, she felt very much at home and she felt privileged to be in the presence of such amazing acting. She was now hungry to find out more and passed by the place as often as she could.

The rain had lessened slightly so Miranda stepped out from the cover of the cloister to gaze up at the ugly gargoyles that stared down at her from the tower of the monastery. A lone black raven circled and searched for a perch. A blast of wind howled around the disused graveyard, forcing one of the side doors to blow open as the rain intensified. She knew this was a way into the Playhouse and it was as if Miranda was receiving an invitation to go into the stage door, even the caw of the raven seemed to cry out that she take the opportunity.

'I can't miss this chance for a quick look backstage, can I?' she reasoned, 'and I'll get soaked to the skin if I don't keep out of the rain.'

But she was still uncertain. It was very rare that she was ever out alone – the City could be a dangerous place for a fourteen year old, even during the day time. If the housekeeper had not been away she would not have needed to collect the fresh loaf of bread that was still warm in her bag. It was this errand that had brought her back here today – being the quickest route to the apothecary where she was staying.

Since the sudden death of her mother a little over a year and a half before, Miranda was often sent to stay at Blackfriars by her father, Thomas. He was a goldsmith in the rich city of St. Albans, just north of London, and as business was very demanding at present he could not always give her the attention she needed. Thomas's brother, Peter, was retired and this gave him enough time to look after Miranda if required whilst new arrangements were made for the family. Thomas knew she enjoyed the breaks in the City of London with her uncle, who had no other close family since the tragic death of his own wife and son during a severe outbreak of the plague many years before. Peter had subsequently not re-married but dedicated his life to the research of herbs, medicine and healing. He had a great interest in Miranda's education and she treated him as a second father, always looking forward to her stays at the apothecary.

'Well, here goes! I hope Uncle Peter won't be cross and I'll only be a few minutes later than he expects. The notice board shows no performances taking place and there would normally be flaming torches at the main entrance if patrons were expected,' she thought.

The door creaked loudly on its rusty old hinges, as Miranda entered the ancient building. A stairway led up to a room on the first floor and there was no sign of anyone. She carefully placed the bag containing the bread on the lowest step and closed the door behind her.

The stone-walled monastery felt very peaceful and quiet and Miranda was able to reflect for a moment on what she was doing. Ever since she could remember she had loved the theatre, and if the morality of the times had allowed, she would certainly have endeavoured to become an actor. But this was 1611 and although not a law, women never challenged the *status quo* – the stage was for men and boys alone.

The closed door rattled as the wind raged outside. It brought her back to the now. With her curiosity mounting, she reached the first floor. An old dusty cobweb brushed across her face, causing her to hesitate. She composed herself and then carried on towards an open door at the end of a short corridor. She looked in.

There was a source of light coming from a window but it was quite dark inside. She ventured further and recoiled at the sight of a monstrous face staring out at her from the back of the room. It did not seem living and her instinct was to stay calm. Miranda realised that the ugly visage was nothing but a mask – a theatre prop of a hideous Grecian god. There was no sound or movement to indicate any other danger, so she entered what she could only presume was a store for some of the properties of the Playhouse.

She marvelled at the range of scenery, strange masks and props that surrounded her. She saw chests marked with owners' details and the titles of plays. 'Possibly these props and costumes are about to be moved,' she thought.

Located halfway up the far wall was a small window through which the faint light entered the room. Miranda wondered if she might see behind the stage and using a chest to stand on, peered through the cracked, stained glass. She could hardly believe her eyes. There in the centre of a room below her, a meeting was taking place.

She marvelled at the range of scenery, strange masks and props

By the light of several large church candles, a group of men, some sat at tables and others standing, were engrossed in work. She wondered what they were doing but presumed that they must be actors accompanied by scribes preparing for a play.

The attention of the group was closely concentrated upon a short, stocky man who seemed to be directing or instructing them. Behind him on the wall was a large map. Miranda knew from her studies that it was of England and the coast of Northern France. It was not common to possess one and the men were obviously wealthy or in service to the King or a nobleman. It was splendidly detailed with beautiful drawings of ships and serpents and rich colours.

Two men who looked like scribes sat at a table surrounded by all sorts of reference books, which were also very rare to possess. Every so often they wrote furiously upon the manuscripts that they each held. Miranda felt she should be afraid but did not seem to feel any trepidation at all. She felt that the actors were somehow friends rather than enemies.

Certain that the actors had not noticed her, she quietly opened the window just a little. She strained to hear their conversation and was intrigued when the name of Agincourt, in France, was mentioned. She heard the man who was directing the group speak of a great battle, and a journey across the sea, which seemed to relate to the map on the wall.

Every so often one of the actors in the group would stand up and give a short speech, or quote a poem or a rhyme. It was a fascinating scene to watch. Then the director went over to the reference books and spoke to the scribes taking notes.

There were two boys sitting either side of a closed door. They sat very quietly as if spellbound by the events unfolding before them. She presumed they were boy actors who worked for the troupe.

Suddenly there was a change in pace and the door opened. The two boys stood up like sentries. A very charismatic looking gentleman in his mid to late forties confidently entered, drawing the attention of the gathering towards him. She presumed that he was a very senior actor or playwright as his face was full of character and depth of experience.

'Who could this be?' she spoke to the air, immediately putting her hand over her mouth, telling herself to be very quiet. The face of the man who entered was somehow familiar to her and she found she was magnetised to him and quite forgot she was trespassing. Observing what was clearly a highly important and private meeting could get her into a great deal of trouble. After a while the actors gathered their rough oak chairs into a circle in response to an invitation from the visitor. They all sat down and fell quiet as if preparing themselves for the next part to begin. The scribes were also invited to sit close by and to bring their manuscripts and pens.

Miranda could not hear clearly what was being said, but was quite taken aback when the actors all began to laugh heartily in response to comments from the visitor. She thought this strange for such an apparently serious gathering. The atmosphere of humorous banter continued until he turned to the scribes. He appeared to tell them some important detail and they eagerly wrote down several lines as quickly as their quill pens could be dipped in the ink. The gathering now became silent as if a matter of more consequence was being discussed and she was intrigued how they appeared to be able to naturally move from joviality to gravity and back again, without difficulty.

As she continued to observe the room, it seemed to her young eyes that since the visitor had entered, the atmosphere appeared to come more alive. The rather dull colours of the green and purple tapestry that hung on the wall opposite her were brighter. The sun streaming in through the high monastery windows, overlooking the lane, cast a spectrum on the rough painted plaster. The group of actors, who at first had seemed to look much the same, seemed now, as she watched, to each reveal their individual characteristics.

One of the two boy players seated by the door caught her attention and she admired his pretty features, his long, slender nose and well-formed face. She thought he must be a player of female roles in the theatre and realised that the room below her was actually the inner stage, with a tiring house behind (this was where actors changed into costume). Through the curtain she could just make out the main stage and the Playhouse beyond, with its high-vaulted ceiling.

As the meeting of the actors continued it was clear that their mutual respect for each other created great warmth and there appeared to be a magic and mysterious glow around everyone. Almost inaudibly the youngest of the actors sat forward and spoke. In response the distinguished looking visitor went over to the map and mused upon it for some time. As he turned, his face showed a fresh and changed expression and to Miranda's perceptive eyes it seemed that the face of king or a nobleman played upon his features like a shimmering mirage.

Miranda had to blink as she thought she must be seeing things. The expression lingered for a few more moments and then disappeared. She thought that if

Through the curtain she could just make out the main stage
and the Playhouse beyond

25

ever she had seen a face with a regal or majestic countenance, then surely this was one.

When the visitor returned to the group one of the youngest actors was asked to join him in the centre of the room. They both stood motionless then quite slowly and to her wonderment, the young man's features altered and his posture changed. It was as if the visitor had transferred to him some power. The youth lost his leanness and appeared to grow broader and older, and a face more fitting a man from the Continent or the Mediterranean danced upon his countenance, as if cast by a light. To her surprise Miranda heard him speak in what sounded, from her experience, to be a very natural French accent and the scribes recorded his words in their manuscripts.

Miranda was still transfixed by the visitor and the majestic countenance once more played upon his face. He stood with his feet firmly planted on the floor wearing a stern expression. He then began to speak in beautifully poetic English, each line rhyming quite naturally. She felt her heartbeat settle as his words soothed her senses. 'This surely is a playwright!' she thought.

Again the scribes with the books wrote down the speech, which she thought must be by a famous king in history that the visitor had committed to memory. She tried to recall the illustrations of the English Kings she had seen in the books at home in St. Albans. Probing in her memory for when she had seen such characteristics in a face, she thought that she must ask her uncle when she returned to the apothecary.

The visitor then unexpectedly looked up towards the props store window and Miranda momentarily looked into his eyes. He made no indication that he had seen her and immediately turned away. For the fleeting moment that their eyes met she felt a wonderful sense of calm and peace.

Unexpectedly the door to the inner stage opened and a further gentleman entered – his ruff and silk cloth jacket indicating he was a knight with a high position at Court. The boys stood up in astonishment, a visiting noble was clearly not expected. All the actors and scribes immediately rose and bowed, as if they were in the presence of the King. They gathered up their things, seeming to know that the knight had come to visit the gentleman who Miranda now presumed to be a member of the King's Men. Once the scribes and actors had left the room the two stood alone facing each other.

Miranda knew that she should not stare, but instantly identified a remarkable resemblance between the two men. She observed that a mutual respect existed between them and they sat down opposite each other at the scribes' table and started what appeared to be a very serious and urgent discussion. She knew that she must leave immediately as their meeting was clearly private. She stepped down from the chest but lost hold of the open window. It made a terribly loud noise as it closed shut, but she was now too far below the opening to see if the two gentlemen's conference had been disturbed.

Miranda rushed out of the room and down the stairs, picked up the loaf of bread that was still on the lowest step and pushed open the door that led to the graveyard. The storm had passed and the sky above was a lovely clear blue as she walked quickly back to the apothecary.

Once back inside, she took off her cloak and tidied her auburn hair and smoothed down her dress. She then took the loaf into the kitchen. Her uncle was in his work room making some medicines for his close friends. She felt she was not yet ready to explain where she had been and Peter instinctively knew this.

'Why not take a rest and we'll talk later?' he asked.

Miranda nodded in agreement.

'Thank you for settling my mind that you are safe,' Peter added as she kissed him on the cheek.

Miranda climbed the stairs to her attic bedroom. She went over to the window and looked down into the lane expecting to see actors from the Playhouse searching for the intruder who had spied upon their gathering. She waited and waited with nervous anticipation, but no men appeared. Eventually she sat down on her bed and regained her composure.

She was convinced that she had been heard at the window of the props store at the Playhouse but rather than this troubling her, she was for some reason possessed with a deep sense of settlement and felt no need to be afraid. She pulled a blanket over herself and slept.

The Face of King Henry V

Later that afternoon Peter came up the stairs and knocked quietly on Miranda's door. She awoke and called out to him and he came into her room. He had been worried by her longer than expected absence.

She was unable to hide a guilty expression, and told him how after picking up the bread she had got caught by the storm and had sheltered by the old monastery. One thing led to another and she took a peek inside and became rather engrossed. Knowing his niece's intense interest in the Playhouse Peter smiled, sure that there was more to her story than she was telling him. He offered to play chess with her that evening, which he knew she enjoyed, in the hope that she would be able to let him know more about what happened. Just as Peter was about to leave the room Miranda asked, 'Uncle, do you have a book in your study of the Kings and Queens of England?'

Peter scratched his chin and thought for a moment, looking like a wizard considering his books of spells. He told her that he was sure he had such a volume and that he would show her after dinner when they sat down to play their game of chess.

After a wash Miranda persisted with her Latin, trying to take her mind off her escapade at the monastery. It was her habit, when concentrating on a text, to play with the gold bracelet, engraved with her name, that her father had given her. She realised that she could not feel it and pulling back the cuff of her blouse was horrified to see that her wrist was bare and the bracelet was missing.

Miranda thought the catch must have opened when she stepped off the chest at the Playhouse and let go of the window overlooking the stage. She pictured the bracelet, with her name upon it, lying upon the floor of the store in the Blackfriars Playhouse. Her imagination ran wild as she became convinced that it would be found and her identity revealed, if the actors enquired in the nearby streets. 'I must go back and retrieve it,' she thought to herself.

She decided she would wait until tomorrow and try once more to get into the old monastery – hoping her bracelet had fallen behind the chest. For now she must not worry.

Soon it was evening. Cathy the housekeeper had returned and she came up to Miranda's room to tell her that dinner was ready. She changed her clothes and on her way down the stairs she was caused to look at the portrait of her uncle's departed wife hanging on the wall. Katherine had been extremely beautiful and Miranda reflected how fragile life was, her own mother having been taken by a fever. She resolved again to never be familiar with each hour and day of life granted to her. The picture took her mind off her concerns over the lost bracelet.

The fire in the hearth crackled in a welcoming way and the candlelight cast a warm glow as she entered her uncle's study. Against the wall there was a small table with several well-polished and glittering objects upon it. There was a fine brass bell with a mahogany handle and an old box with engravings of mythical creatures upon it. A small statue of a griffin made of silver stood next to Uncle Peter's papers like a guardian. In the corner there was a chessboard with the pieces already set out for their game. The low ceiling beams and pictures on the wall made the room seem like the abode of a magician high up in a castle in some mysterious kingdom.

After dinner, the evening's cold made Miranda and her uncle draw close to the fire and they played several games of chess together. She thought dreamily about the afternoon's adventure and wondered if she should tell him the truth about her visit to the Blackfriars monastery. Peter, fetching the book she had asked to see, brought her back to the present.

'Here it is, my dear,' he said, handing the book to her. 'This is a very rare volume with some portraits of the Kings and Queens of England.'

Miranda looked through the book with Peter's help until she came to a picture entitled *King Henry V at the Battle of Agincourt*.

She could not hide her astonishment as there before her was the face she had seen that afternoon at the

Playhouse. It had been portrayed, as realistically as if it had been King Henry V himself. The face of the member of the King's Men, who had become the focus of attention for the gathering of actors, had been transformed before her eyes. Peter asked her if there was anything wrong. She apologised for her strange reaction and then told him everything that had happened at the Playhouse. She went through all that she had seen from the scribes working with the map and the books and to the arrival of the man who she presumed was a member of the King's Men. Peter listened intently and without interruption, but when Miranda described who she thought was a knight or lord, he stopped her account abruptly.

'What's wrong, Uncle?' Miranda asked, very concerned at the grave expression on his face.

'Please go over again what you observed during those last few minutes.'

Miranda conveyed as best she could the commotion caused by the knight's arrival and all that she could remember about his appearance and facial features. She recounted how she had observed the mutual respect that appeared to exist between the two men and that a private conference followed. She explained that it was at this point that she left the props store, not wishing to observe any more.

'You must not tell anyone about this,' Uncle Peter said as she finished. 'I know that the knight concerned maintains a strict anonymity where his connections with the King's Men and the Blackfriars are concerned. As a patron of the Playhouse I will explain how you came to be there, should it ever be necessary.'

'Can you let me know the identity of the visitor who I presumed was a member of the King's Men?' Miranda asked.

'Yes, that I can tell you. This afternoon, my dear, you saw the eminent actor and playwright William Shakespeare. Although nearly retired, he finds any excuse to come back to the Playhouse and you were lucky indeed to see him,' he said, pausing. 'Please remember what I said – never tell anyone about this.'

Miranda nodded and went upstairs to bed, as her uncle put away the chess set and the books.

In her room Miranda thought hard about the bracelet she had left behind in the Playhouse. She had not told Peter about its loss, as she did not want to alarm him any further, but knew that she must do something to recover it. She was however concerned about the way her uncle had reacted to the account of what she witnessed from the props store.

* * *

When Miranda awoke the next day, she had only one thing on her mind – to return to the monastery and the props store. The thought played upon her mind during her morning's study and she was relieved when it was lunchtime. She slipped quietly down the steps, went out of the back entrance, ran along the side alley and into the lane. The weather was much kinder and the wind had died away. Within minutes she was once more outside the monastery. She followed the path through the graveyard and was relieved to find the door was still not locked.

'Had she not been heard?' she thought to herself, hardly believing that she was so fortunate.

Miranda was soon again at the foot of the rough stone steps leading up to the room from where she had observed the meeting. Climbing more confidently up the stairs she peered inside the store, already prepared to face the Grecian mask that still stared out into the hallway. All seemed very much as before as she quietly walked over to the chest upon which she had stood to observe the actors. She could not believe her good fortune, for there next to the leather casing her gold bracelet lay gleaming on the floor. Miranda knelt down, picked it up and quietly murmured a grateful prayer to God. Turning to leave and rejoicing at her luck, she was once again gripped by curiosity.

As quiet as a mouse she climbed up to where she had stood the day before and peered through the corner of the glass window. A curtain had been drawn and she could see the main stage area, which was being carefully prepared for what appeared to be an important event. Large church candles stood on a fine oak table and there were several trunks and other tables, chairs and books arranged neatly. She could not see any of the actors, and although she wished she could stay, she knew it would be more sensible to leave. She climbed down and turned to go. It was then that her heart missed a beat. There were at least two people climbing up the stone stairs. She could hear clearly the sound of their footsteps and laughter.

As if by instinct Miranda opened the chest and saw various garments inside. She rummaged through the assorted clothes, made a space large enough for her to hide and climbed in. Once inside, she put her hand up through the jackets, scarves and ruffs and closed the lid on top of her. The cracks in the old timber gave her enough air to breathe.

From what she could hear from her hiding place, two men who were in hearty conversation had entered the small room and were moving amongst the costumes

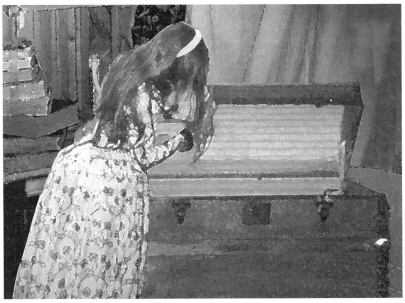

Miranda opened the chest and saw various garments inside

and the props. Her fear was somewhat lessened by the gentle manner in which the men went about their business, but still she braced herself for the moment when the chest might be opened and her presence revealed. For several more minutes the sound of the men moving in the store continued. Miranda heard the men's voices, as they stood right over her hiding place.

She held her breath, ready to be discovered, and then to her amazement felt the chest being lifted. This was followed by the sound of shuffling feet and footsteps as she was carried down the steps into the lane. The men were obviously strong and did not comment on the extra weight of these particular props!

'Oh, no, what is going to happen to me?' she thought as she let out a small sob. She held her bracelet tight and closed her eyes.

Miranda Calls her Name

Back at the apothecary, Peter was becoming genuinely worried for his niece's safety. A fresh layer of sleet was thick on the ground as he came into the lane outside, rubbing his arms to warm himself. He knew he must search for her and scolded himself for not having been more vigilant. He had seen her leave by the back stairs, but he had not said anything or interfered. But this excitement over the Playhouse may get her into serious trouble.

He walked to the old monastery where the Blackfriars was located and soon found the graveyard and covered cloister that Miranda had described to him. By coincidence the well-known theatre owner and friend of William Shakespeare, Mr. Burbage, was leaving the side entrance, locking the door behind him.

He recognised Miranda's uncle as a patron of the Playhouse and greeted him.

'Good afternoon sir. It is Peter, the apothecary, isn't it? Greetings.'

'My dear Mr. Burbage, I am so glad you are here. I...'

'You look very worried Peter. Is anything wrong?'

He briefly told the story of Miranda's visit to the Playhouse and her escapade in the props store. Without hesitation Mr. Burbage reopened the door and they both went up the stairs to see if Miranda was there. Not finding her, they returned to the cloister and cemetery, circling the monastery until they came to the main entrance of the Playhouse. Steep steps led up to large oak doors within a Gothic arch. Entering the building they climbed the winding staircase that led up to the main theatre hall.

The great chamber that once housed the refectory for the monks felt almost like a cathedral as they entered. Peter stopped for a moment and looked up at the high-vaulted ceiling, the galleries of seats and three levels of staging. Despite the worry he had for his niece's safety, he was awed for a moment by the majestic setting that had been chosen for the finest

Steep steps led up to large oak doors within a Gothic arch

indoor theatre in the whole of London. He then brought his attention back to his present concerns for Miranda's whereabouts.

At that very moment three actors brought a chest and other props onto the stage. Miranda was hiding inside, too afraid to utter a sound.

Mr. Burbage and Peter climbed up onto the stage and asked the actors if they had seen a young girl of Miranda's description in the Playhouse. They shook their heads and replied that they would have certainly recalled such an unusual occurrence.

'Could I ask what this chest and props are to be used for?' asked Peter.

'They are for us to rehearse with William Shakespeare and make preparations for his latest work, *The Tempest*. There are still some scenes to be completed and characters to be defined,' replied one actor.

'It is a very special occasion, as this is the most eagerly awaited play he has yet written,' added another.

'Its first performance will be in front of King James later this year. Those close to William Shakespeare believe that the play is not only a great work of poetry and theatre, but contains a profound theology for the salvation of the King's subjects in this great land of England. Rich or poor, aristocrat or labourer, there is a message for all in this story!' the third actor said, clearly inspired by the work.

Peter nodded, appreciating the actors' views about the play, totally unaware how near he was to his niece.

Miranda gripped the bracelet tight in her hiding place within the chest. She felt very uncomfortable about not shouting out, but was unable to utter a word.

* * *

Outside in the lane Peter asked Mr. Burbage to walk with him to the apothecary. He told him that for some unknown reason he felt sure Miranda was not in any danger. He did not know why he felt his niece was safe, but it was a strong instinct. He was convinced that she was still in the Playhouse.

'If we hear no news we shall return within the hour,' Mr. Burbage said reassuringly as they arrived.

Once inside Peter's study, Cathy prepared hot drinks for them both. The two men sat by the fire and continued their discussion.

'Do you know more about this new play, *The*

Tempest?' Peter asked. 'I could not help but be intrigued by what the actors said.'

'As you know the theatre company carries the King's personal seal, and is the most highly trained group of actors in England, and no doubt Europe, at this time. Although nearing retirement, William Shakespeare is a highly skilled actor and still the principal playwright of the company. Young Miranda, your niece, is one of the few persons ever to have witnessed one of their private meetings. Scribes were editing notes and preparations were taking place for a performance of *The Life of King Henry Fifth*. The play was written some years ago and is being revised for a special presentation to King James. It is of interest to him at the moment, as he faces fresh challenges from abroad and seeks inspiration from the play. As you know, it shows in such a noble and passionate way, the great defeat of the French by King Henry V and his army. If your niece had stayed longer at the Playhouse, she would also have observed preparations for the new play, *The Tempest*.'

Peter listened intently.

'What is little known outside a small circle of people is the process by which many of our plays are produced.

William Shakespeare and sometimes a co-writer create and prepare much of the text first, and then the characters are further developed by the troupe. The actors experience each part of the story, as if they are the living person in the play – whether in medieval England, ancient Rome, Greece or Egypt or upon far distant islands. They become like time travellers and they are sometimes called Mummers. To assist, other members of the troupe provide the historical reference and setting, whilst trained writers act as scribes and take down every word that they speak. It is quite fantastic and remarkable and sometimes frightening, to witness characters and scenes from the past brought to life before one's eyes. Some say it is as if the person from history is incarnating once more – quite extraordinary. This not only includes speeches, but specific characteristics, features and occurrences never recorded in the history books. This is how it has been possible for plays of such an incredibly diverse origin and rich history to be developed over a relatively short time.' Mr Burbage paused.

'I knew something of how the plays were written, but never imagined that the method involved so much of a magical or what could be called supernatural process,' Peter reflected.

'Now I will briefly move on to the preparations for the play *The Tempest*. I can say little, as there is much secrecy around the production and the story has been inspired by a prominent thinker and philosopher close to the King. It tells of the deep goodness of a nobleman who has been wronged by his brother and exiled upon an enchanted island with his beautiful daughter. Through his mastery of good magic a tempest is raised at his command by a spirit in service to him. Those who were his enemies in the past are watched over by the spirit and brought safely ashore. Gradually and mysteriously through the enchantment of the island, they are all re-united and the wrongs of the past settled. His daughter finds true love and with her father they are restored to their rightful royal position on returning home. But the play is also an allegory for us all to contemplate. There are many messages in the play for the audience to take from it, if they desire.' Mr. Burbage fell silent.

'I wonder how *The Tempest* will be introduced, when it is presented to King James at Court?' Peter thought. It was well known to him that the King was searching continually for new meaning to religion and was a great supporter of the theatre, music and arts. He had even commissioned Sir Francis Bacon, the man whose identity he could not reveal to his niece after her observation of the meeting at the Blackfriars, to lead a group of scholars to create a specially revised Bible.

'Thank you, Mr. Burbage,' Peter broke the silence. 'It sounds as if William Shakespeare has written a special contemplation for the King and us all, on the meaning of life!'

* * *

Meanwhile, at the Blackfriars Playhouse the actors had all left the stage. Miranda took the opportunity to lift the lid of the chest to peer out. She was grateful for a few moments of relief from the confinement of her hiding place, and the garments pressing down upon her. She climbed out of the chest and looked towards the empty auditorium, imagining it full of theatre goers on an opening night. She bowed to the imaginary audience.

The sound of footsteps and voices echoing in the adjoining hallway indicated that the actors were coming back onto the stage. She returned to her hiding place, ducked back down under the clothes and carefully lowered the lid of the chest. She waited in silence.

Soon there was the sound of a table being moved and chairs being set in place, as if a whole group were within a few feet of her.

'Gentlemen,' a stern-sounding man began. 'We have gathered for a further discussion concerning the forthcoming production of *The Tempest*. This is a very special play and possibly the finest we have ever staged. Not just an historical drama, but a tale of justice and how goodness prevails over evil, allowing those wronged to regain their rightful birthright. As the plot may still be new to some of you, we shall recount the tale.'

Miranda lay absolutely still and listened in wonder.

A lively sounding character, who was the troupe's jester, took up the story, making the setting of the play come to life.

'There is a distant and deserted island in the sea, whereupon live two castaways – a nobleman called Prospero and his teenage daughter. The island was intended as a place of exile or even death, when they were left there by his evil brother. However this isle provided the means for their survival, shelter and protection. A place of enchantment indeed as our play will show!'

Miranda listened intently and pictured the island as he spoke; it was as if she could feel the tropical heat and hear the waves crashing upon the shore, with a bright yellow sun and clear blue sky above.

The jester continued.

'Prospero's daughter came to the island at such a young age, that she has no memory of having seen another human face, other than her father's. They live in a cave, hewn out of rock, divided into several rooms – one of which is Prospero's study, full of his books of magic and alchemy. Through sorcery he releases good spirits, natural to the island, that up to this time were imprisoned by a witch, named Sycorax. The chief amongst these spirits is Ariel, a fairy of the air, and now a servant of Prospero. The use of magic by Prospero is a desperate attempt to save his family, for he has no desire to be a sorcerer.'

Miranda thought of her uncle at the apothecary shop and his room with the fire, the chessboard and books. She was so lost in what she was hearing that she forgot the danger she was in, hiding in the chest.

A different actor continued with the story.

'The evil witch Sycorax has a son – a beast-like man called Caliban. Prospero has tried, but to no avail, to educate him. He lets the monster live with his family as a servant. As if by fate, destiny brings a ship close by the island with the King of Naples, his son and Prospero's evil brother on board. Among the travellers is also the kind man who helped Prospero with books and provisions when they were first cast away. Prospero, with the help of the spirit Ariel, raises a storm. The power of his magic can easily sink the ship, drowning all on board, but Prospero has no intention of doing them harm. He takes steps through Ariel to bring them safely to shore and over the next few days all the castaways fall under the spell of the Enchanted Island. The King's son Ferdinand falls in love with Prospero's daughter and the wrongs of the past are set to right. They are honourably returned to Naples, where she becomes Queen. Prospero releases Ariel and finally Prospero discards his magic forever.'

Miranda was nearly in tears, never having heard a story so wonderful in her life. Completely lost in her dreams, she imagined herself the daughter of Prospero.

'How wonderful it would be to fall in love with the King's son on the Enchanted Island and become the Queen of Naples,' she thought.

'We have an important issue to resolve. How shall we present the character of Prospero's daughter? What is her name?' a senior actor asked. There was a long silence as the actors and scribes considered his questions.

Still no one spoke. Suddenly there was a voice that came as if from nowhere.

'Miranda!'

The actors were startled. The name was spoken as if from the ether.

Miranda was so lost in her imaginings about the magical island that she spoke out her name clearly and with a curious power in her voice.

The actors looked at each other mystified.

One actor addressed the boy player who was cast as Prospero's daughter in the new production.

'Did you speak, Nathan?'

'Not I, sir!' replied Nathan. The group remained silent.

''Tis Miranda?' The young man playing Ferdinand, the King's son, asked quizzically, as if to an unseen being. 'Speak again!'

The room remained silent. Miranda was too afraid to utter another word.

The group was now impatient to solve the mystery of the voice and a stern-looking actor with bright ginger hair went over to the chest and opened the lid. He pulled the garments out and stared in amazement as Miranda appeared.

To the surprise of the assembled actors, a real, living girl, well dressed with a winter cloak, rose from the chest. Standing fully upright she looked as if she had risen from the trapdoor in the stage floor or had materialised like a genie, summoned by the actors.

Miranda's appearance caused great consternation amongst the actors. They were, after all, the famous and elite King's Men, and females were not usually allowed to be seen with them on stage, not even in a rehearsal. They stared at her in disbelief.

The stern-looking actor was about to escort Miranda from the Playhouse, when the door to the inner stage opened dramatically and there stood William Shakespeare – the great playwright himself. Everything and everyone froze.

A Game of Chess on the Stage

*M*iranda came to her senses and was acutely aware that she should not be on the stage. William Shakespeare, however, seemed genuinely amused by the situation and interested only in how the young lady had spirited herself so successfully into a gathering of the august King's Men. If this was a grave state of affairs for her to be in, William Shakespeare made no sign or indication of any displeasure. In fact, his reaction was quite the opposite.

At William Shakespeare's request, she was helped out of the chest and given a high-back chair. The playwright had an incredible gift for remembering faces and he knew he had seen Miranda before. He then recalled the occasion when he had looked up at the window above the tiring house during a scribes meeting and saw a young lass observing them. 'So this is the same girl?' he thought.

He did not believe in coincidence, instead choosing to see everything as part of an interconnected story. He was determined to discover why Miranda was now part of their play.

Before anything else took place, William Shakespeare asked for a message to be sent to Miranda's uncle, to tell him that his niece was safe. He knew Peter as a dedicated patron of the theatre, and had used his services as an apothecary on several occasions. A boy player was instructed to leave immediately and bring Peter to the Playhouse.

Miranda sat rather nervously in the chair, as the playwright asked her to tell the story how she had come to be in this incredible situation. Initially the actors were very serious, but they soon joined William Shakespeare as he laughed heartily at her story. This was the kind of humour that had caught Miranda's attention when she first witnessed their work from the props store.

William Shakespeare pondered the situation. Throughout his life he had always followed his instinct and believed deeply in fate. He was sure the apothecary's niece had appeared on his stage to bring the character to life.

He also liked the name Miranda. It conjured up the far distant island of Tenerife, from where it originated. He had followed the news of the discovery of the Bermudas by the British and the conquering of the Canaries by the Spanish with great interest.

'So, are we agreed that this young lady has shown the spirit of the heroine of our play, *The Tempest*?' William Shakespeare addressed the group. The men all nodded, still somewhat in disbelief. Not only was it improper for a girl to be onstage, but for her to be in the midst of the King's Men as well, was almost unthinkable.

'And what about you, young Nathan, what do you think? You may indeed be acting this very part one day soon.'

Miranda turned and saw it was the boy whose lovely face and fine features she had admired yesterday as he sat by the door. In the very instant that William Shakespeare addressed him, his features seemed to subtly change and she thought she was seeing her own face in a mirror.

'The name Miranda would be most suitable for our heroine, sir. And this young lady demonstrates her qualities well!' Nathan spoke firmly and politely. Miranda beamed and wished she could speak more to him – he was the most charming boy she had ever seen.

'Well said, Nathan!' There was a kindness in William Shakespeare's voice.

Miranda's character reminded him of his eldest daughter, Susannah, and he was now settled to her name being used in the play.

'It is a shame that the wont of our age prohibits your participation in our play as an actor, but we can stretch the rules a little today!' William Shakespeare said, making a small bow towards her. She was almost in tears as a small table was brought on stage and was asked to sit down opposite the actor who would be playing the Prince of Naples.

'Miranda,' said William Shakespeare softly, as she looked intently at the young actor. 'Please meet Ferdinand, the son of the King. He has by fate been brought safely to the shores of your island.'

She looked into the face of the young man and gradually, imperceptibly at first, the slender English qualities of his features appeared to transform. His pale complexion took on an olive glow. The characteristics of his skin melted and softened, as if a native of the Mediterranean.

She no longer felt the chill of England's winter in the presence of the young man, and looked into the face of the Prince of Naples. While still spellbound, she became softened and freer. She no longer felt the restrictions of the severe dress that she wore or the collar that was tight around her neck. Gradually she felt her own skin yield to the warmth that she felt inside her and she was transformed into a young princess.

She had not noticed two scribes with books and pens making notes, while an artist was sketching the scene in charcoal. On the upper stage a group of musicians, who had so far been silent, now began to play, in harmony with the tranquillity of the setting. Miranda looked up and it seemed as if the angels in heaven had suddenly appeared to play their music.

Within the quietness and stillness of the atmosphere that now surrounded the two people, William Shakespeare mused on the scene before him. The music continued and the young man's face still shone with the warmth of a distant land. William Shakespeare's face brightened as an idea entered his alert and exploring mind.

He spoke quietly to one of the actors, who softly tiptoed out of the room and returned with a chess set. Without disturbing the setting, the playwright placed a board between Ferdinand and Miranda. He positioned

He positioned certain pieces as if making a game

59

certain pieces as if making a game, and then stepped back. Needing no instructions, the two began to play.

At that moment Miranda's uncle arrived with Mr. Burbage, having received the message that his niece was safe and well and at the Playhouse. Quietly standing at the front of the theatre, he saw, to his great surprise, Miranda seated on the stage surrounded by the King's Men. She appeared to be the central character and Peter had never seen her look so beautiful before. It was then that he realised that not only was his niece acting on a public stage, but they were also in the presence of the King's Men. He could not understand why Miranda and he were not in some trouble. William Shakespeare assured Peter that all was well and that his niece was playing a very useful role for him.

For at least an hour William Shakespeare and the King's Men worked with Miranda and the young actor creating more scenes for the two to play. They were particularly impressed with her ease in taking up the part of Prospero's daughter and how she was not at all overawed by the stage or the other actors.

Peter watched in a trance as the scene was completed. One by one the King's Men bowed as Miranda left the stage. Seeing her uncle she ran over to give him a big hug.

'Your niece's courage and good fortune led her to be a contributor to a very magical scene in our play. I am sure she will explain all to you later,' William Shakespeare said, giving Miranda back her cloak.

'We must still debate the name that your niece has brought to the character, but she has added greatly to the role by her exceptional and natural acting ability.' Turning to her he bowed. 'I am afraid you must now leave, we have much to complete in private.'

Miranda walked slowly with Peter through the streets to the apothecary. Inside they were soon warming themselves by the large log fire in the study and Cathy brought some hot soup and bread. Miranda looked around the room vacantly, seeing the chess set in the corner and her uncle's collection of books. She thought she could hear the sound of the sea washing upon the shore of the Enchanted Island of castaways. She then told him the tale of how she had arrived upon the stage.

A Surprise Visitor

Miranda amused herself in the attic room, writing a letter to cousin Jane, whilst looking out of the window at the skyline of snow-covered rooftops. There was a knock on her door and her uncle looked in with a smile.

'Miranda, you have a visitor,' he said.

'Who is it?' she asked excitedly, putting down her quill. Peter put a finger to his lips and motioned for her to follow him. Intrigued by his secrecy she became a little nervous. She smoothed down her dress and tidied her hair to settle herself before following him downstairs. When they reached the hall he asked her to go into the study and meet her visitor. He called Cathy to bring them all warm mead.

Inside she saw a figure standing in front of the fire warming his hands, but could not make out who it was. Her visitor turned as her footsteps made a sound on the stone floor. It was then that she recognised his slender features and the sweet face that had assured his popularity as a boy player.

'Nathan!'

He now faced her with a broad smile on his face.

'Please excuse my unexpected visit, Miranda, but I felt I had to meet you in person, away from the Playhouse!' Nathan smiled again. 'And to tell you that because of your great interest in the theatre, William Shakespeare would like you to know more about our work. Should you be interested, he wants me to be your guide at the Playhouse and to show you all and everything about the theatre and the boy actors. He also asked me to give you this.' He reached inside his coat and took out a small parcel.

She did not know what to say. Within the fine blue material she discovered a small volume printed on rough paper. She opened the folio carefully and was able to read the title page. She noted the date of publication, 1604.

The Tragicall Historie of Hamlet Prince of Denmarke
By William Shakespeare
Newly imprinted and enlarged to almost as much
againe as it was, according to the true
and perfect coppie.

'It is a folio of the complete parts for the play performed by the King's Men,' Nathan explained. 'It is quite rare and you must have impressed William Shakespeare greatly!'

'I shall write to him to express my great thanks when I return home to St. Albans later this week.'

Cathy brought in the hot drinks, leaving the two alone. Peter had already excused himself and was back in his workroom.

Nathan looked around Miranda's uncle's study, at the chessboard, the books and the open fire. It reminded him of Prospero's cave on the Enchanted Island. For a moment he could not separate the girl that sat next to him from the one who had appeared upon the stage from the chest. He knew that should he ever take the part in the play *The Tempest* in the future, 'Miranda' would never be just a name.

It reminded him of Prospero's cave on the Enchanted Island

Part Two

Summer 1611

The King's Ghost

A heavy summer shower drummed upon the roof of an old shop in Blackfriars and streaks of water ran down the thick glass windows.

'It always seems to be raining these days!' Peter thought, sat as usual at his desk surrounded by books and jars of herbs in a room that looked like a magician's den. Miranda played a lute in the music room next door, and was once more in his charge, as her father was away trading in gold and other jewels for the business. Each time she visited he ensured that there was a lute for her to play in her room. The fashion for playing instruments had developed when Queen Elizabeth first favoured this pursuit many years before.

Since her mother's death Peter encouraged Miranda in these pursuits, sure that a love of drama, literature and an ability to play music would always provide her with

The fashion for playing instruments had developed when Queen Elizabeth first favoured this pursuit

opportunities, friends and an escape from loneliness. He tapped his fingers lightly on his desk in time with a tune she was playing by John Dowland. The famous composer was not known for jovial music, yet the piece was unusually bright and he hummed contentedly to himself.

A radiant beam of sunshine broke through the dark rain clouds and delightfully illuminated a large crystal hanging in the music room window. Miranda watched as a rainbow of coloured flashes danced around the wooden panelling. She laid down the lute and mused for a moment upon the new state of affairs in her life. Everything seemed more magical since her chance meeting with William Shakespeare and the King's Men players. In their special world, wonder was not as uncommon as it had previously seemed to be for her.

'Can I stay forever in this adventure?' she thought to herself. She might never act upon the stage of the theatre, the custom of the age preventing this, but she was determined never to be separated from the astonishing enchantment she had discovered.

The apothecary door opened and a large bag, soaked with rain, landed on the floorboards with a thump –

leaving a small puddle. The arrival of Miranda's cousin Jane momentarily disturbed the monastic quiet of the apothecary, where the herbs, ointments and mixtures kept in cracked, glazed jars stood in silence on their shelves. The intense beauty of Jane's face and her long, raven black hair were unmistakeable. Peter stood up with a smile, having forgotten that she was staying with them. There was an outbreak of the Black Death in her home city of Rochester and although London was often affected, it was safer at present in Blackfriars. Miranda and Jane were nearly the same age, great friends as well as cousins. Uncle Peter said that the two girls brought out the mischief in each other.

'Isn't it wonderful that we are both here in the Old City?' Miranda said as she helped her cousin carry the large bag up the steep wooden stairs. The steps smelt of beeswax and Jane felt comforted by the familiar surroundings of the apothecary. Old paintings and sketches lined the plastered walls and on the very top landing there was an old faded tapestry of a knight in armour. The only part of it that retained its clarity and colour were the two piercing eyes of the nobleman.

'Good afternoon, Sir Topas!' Jane said cheekily,

as she gazed at the knight. 'A pleasure to be visiting you again!'

Settled into the attic room, which overlooked the city streets, Miranda opened the small leaded window for her cousin. Jane marvelled at the great wooden tower of St. Paul's Cathedral – only a few streets away across a great square. It was now early evening and the sky was streaked with purple and orange. Miranda pointed out the monastery where she had experienced her first encounter with the King's Men. Jane was aware of her meeting with William Shakespeare from the letter Miranda's father had brought during a visit and was keen to find out more. The setting sun cast a fading light show upon the ancient building and the tightly crowded rows of buildings nearby. They both breathed in the excitement of the City before catching up on their news.

'What is William Shakespeare like in person? I know so little about him,' Jane asked, as she munched a freshly baked oat biscuit.

'If you remember from my letter I was on stage with the King's Men during a rehearsal of his new play, *The Tempest*. He was wonderfully considerate and courteous towards me, even though I should have been expelled from the theatre as soon as they found me hiding in a chest!'

'Hiding in a chest? I did not know about that bit of the story. What have you been up to?' Jane asked.

'It was very embarrassing really, although it gave me the most incredible opportunity to be in the presence of these amazing actors. I also met Nathan, a boy actor who will be playing the part of Miranda in the new play.'

'Would any boy players like me, do you think?'

'I am sure they would, but with over 300 plays being put on around the town this year they do not have much time for us girls. Nathan is working hard to be accepted as an apprentice to the King's Men and they rehearse night and day at this time of the year.'

'That is a shame!'

'Yes, but I hope we can visit the Playhouse again soon.'

'Why is that?'

'I think William Shakespeare was quite impressed by my interest in his plays. I know I can never be an actor, but he was keen that I know more about their work.'

'What is that?' Jane asked, pointing at a small volume on the table.

'That is one of only a few copies of one of his plays in

existence. Mr. Shakespeare gave it to me as a gift after I helped with the chess game scene from *The Tempest*.' Miranda picked up the small book made up of roughly printed sheets and passed it to her cousin.

'*Hamlet*. What a curious name. I have never heard of this play. When was it published?'

'This folio dates from 1604. Uncle Peter has seen it performed at the Playhouse and I study the verse every night – learning as much of it as I can.'

Jane sensed that the little book she held in her hand had a special significance.

'Do you know any of the lines that you could act out for me?'

Miranda hesitated, considering her cousin's request.

'There is a really creepy part about a ghost – the appearance of Prince Hamlet's own father held in purgatory before departing for heaven or hell. Peter helped me learn the part as the phantom walks the dark ramparts of the great Castle of Elsinore in Denmark,' Miranda explained, pausing before setting the scene.

'It is night time and the castle is shrouded in thick mist. Soldiers on high ramparts keep watch.' The room seemed to turn a little chilly as she spoke. Jane wrapped herself in her shawl, pulled her knees up to her chin and listened with intense concentration. Miranda continued to conjure up the supernatural atmosphere befitting this part of the play.

'The pale shimmering ghost appears out of the mist and walks towards Hamlet. The spirit wants to lead the young prince to some unknown destination and Hamlet resists. He calls out to the foul spectre, as if it will take his life:

Hamlet: *Whither wilt thou lead me? Speak!*
I'll go no further.
Ghost: *Mark me.*
Hamlet: *I will.*
Ghost: *My hour is almost come*
When I to sulphurous and tormenting flames
Must render up myself.
Hamlet: *Alas, poor ghost.*
Ghost: *Pity me not, but lend thy serious hearing*
To what I shall unfold.
Hamlet: *Speak, I am bound to hear.*
Ghost: *So art thou to revenge when thou shalt hear.*
Hamlet: *What?*
Ghost: *I am thy father's spirit,*

Doomed for a certain term to walk the night
And for the day confined to fast in fires
Till the foul crimes done in my days of nature
Are burnt and purged away. But that I am forbid
To tell the secrets of my prison-house
I could a tale unfold whose lightest word
Would harrow up thy soul, freeze thy young blood,
Make thy two eyes like stars start from their spheres,
Thy knotted and combined locks to part
And each particular hair to stand on end...

Miranda paused. A little further on through the lines she began to read again.

Ghost: *Revenge his foul and most unnatural murder.*
Hamlet: *Murder!*
Ghost: *Murder most foul...'*

Jane sat in stunned silence. The room felt as if a real ghost had walked across the floor.

'Whose murder is to be avenged?' she asked, in a hushed voice.

'The King's own brother has poisoned him while he slept, with the intention of marrying his wife the queen, and taking the throne by evil deceit,' Miranda replied with a grave voice. 'But enough, it is time for sleep.'

'I am not sure I can after that tale!'

The two girls fetched a taper from the kitchen and lit the candles on their bedside tables, making the attic room glow orange. There was a painting of a group of actors on the wall; the players seeming to come to life in the half-light. The girls both sensed that a magical time lay ahead. Little did they know just how special it would turn out to be.

The Blackfriars Crypt

*N*ext morning Miranda and Jane made their way down from the attic room to where Peter waited to greet them with a message.

'Well, this is surely an eventful day! Some patrons and friends of the Blackfriars Playhouse have been invited to a party this evening and I can of course take my two wonderful nieces.'

The two girls beamed with delight.

'Is there a new play already or is a performance of *The Tempest* planned?' Miranda asked.

'I am not sure, but after music practice this afternoon, Cathy will help you both get ready,' Peter replied.

Later, whilst the two girls played their lutes in the

garden room, Peter instructed Cathy to choose dresses for his nieces. He went to his workroom to complete a herbal remedy for William Shakespeare. The playwright's digestion troubled him a great deal these days. Peter encouraged him to rest more, but to little effect.

At six in the evening, Peter walked with his nieces towards the Blackfriars. He was visibly proud of Miranda and Jane. He realised they were growing up quickly. They were quite lovely in their fine dresses, and at fourteen were already fine young ladies in the making.

As they approached, the outline of the ancient monastery looked like a medieval castle against the violet sky. Ravens from the fearful Tower of London perched upon the gruesome gargoyles that surveyed the cobbled lanes from each corner. Miranda imagined the black-cloaked monks, who had walked the cold stone floors before Henry VIII banished them. Within the crypt and monastic rooms they had lived, prayed and slept. The once holy place was now the home for the most talked about Playhouse in the City, whose patrons included the elite of London's society.

The three arrived at the entrance and Miranda pointed out the carved griffin embossed in stone above the door to her cousin. The mythical beast was on many buildings nearby and was said to be the guardian of the City Fathers, and of London's wealth.

A brightly dressed jester opened the imposing oak front door on their arrival. He was a mute, his face pockmarked from childhood illness and he greeted them by ringing several of the bells sewn onto his tunic. They were then ushered into a hallway by a boy actor of the company. Miranda now knew that they were affectionately called *playboys*. This one was dressed as a servant to Cleopatra, the queen of Egypt. Other boy actors, dressed as characters from the plays of the King's Men, mingled with the guests.

Miranda was awed once again by the Playhouse. She remembered her own adventure in the props store above the tiring house and her time on the stage in the rehearsals for *The Tempest*. Half in a dream, she wandered about the hallway looking at the pictures on the walls and staring up at the carved cornice, once part of the old monastery, that depicted scenes from the lives of the twelve apostles. Nathan appeared from behind a pillar and bumped into her. She froze on the spot – it was as if she was looking into a mirror. He was dressed in a richly finished Grecian costume.

'Are you in costume for the part of Miranda?' she asked.

'I cannot say, as I am in role! It is the rule. I can tell you later, but not now,' he said, putting a finger to his lips. 'Why are you staring at me?'

'How can you look so much like me? Is it the costume you are wearing or is it something else?'

'As we are becoming friends I won't try to be clever and all mysterious with you. We are trained in mime and more difficult skills known to the King's Men, such as how to give oneself fully to the character in the play, and I am always practising!' Nathan gave a cheeky grin. He bowed and then disappeared along the corridor.

In an adjoining room four musicians entertained the visitors with songs and tunes by William Shakespeare's musical producer, Robert Johnson. There were rumours that Johnson might even attend. Food and drinks were set out on a table – veal, rabbit, hare and pigeon with large chunks of bread, ale, mead and wine. There were actors from other theatre companies with their wives and some important looking people wearing richly coloured clothes.

There was a sense of expectancy in the air. A holy man dressed in a white hooded robe entered the room.

Wearing a long beard and carrying a stick he looked a little out of place. Miranda was not sure what play the character was from and no one gave him a second glance. He stood in a corner and read a small leather bound book with what appeared to be a Celtic cross on the cover, and then made his way through the throng.

'William Shakespeare!' Miranda exclaimed, realising that he had come into the room in costume. He put his finger to his lips as he walked past; approaching a group of rich merchants and Miranda heard them gasp in surprise at his costume.

'I did not know that William Shakespeare was fascinated by the Monks and Druids of Ancient Briton,' Miranda said to Peter.

'He will do anything to help raise funds for the theatre! Wealthy guests love to see him dress up – it reminds them of all the wonderful plays being performed here, like *Cymbeline*.'

'I haven't heard that title before. What is it about?'

'Not everyone likes the story, but in my humble opinion it contains some of his finest prose. It is set in Ancient Briton and Rome and it interested me immensely because of how you arrived on the stage during the rehearsals of the King's Men. It reminded me of a scene in the play.'

'Really?'

'There is a scene when a deceitful character in the story uses a chest to gain entry to the leading character Imogen's room.'

Miranda remembered how she had lost her bracelet and hid in a chest in the props store at the Playhouse and was intrigued that it mirrored the play.

'Was I deceitful when I hid in the props store?'

'In a way you were. But all is now forgiven,' he replied with a smile.

'Uncle, can we see that play?' Miranda asked, now curious about what happens to Imogen.

'We will wait and see when, if ever, it is performed again! As I said, many people dislike the story, but there was a memorable performance earlier this year here at the Blackfriars and I consider Imogen as one of William Shakespeare's finest heroines,' he replied.

William Shakespeare came over to Peter, his indigestion troubling him again.

'My son-in-law in Stratford is always giving me some potion or another,' he said.

This prompted Peter to take out the herbs he had prepared for him. 'These may help when mixed with warm water,' he said and he placed the parcel on an oak table.

'Thank you, Peter, I shall take it regularly whilst I am here in the City and I appreciate your concern!'

Peter and the playwright continued to talk while Jane and Miranda asked permission to leave the room. They found themselves in a long corridor with several doors. At the end was a staircase that led up to the first floor.

'Why don't we see if there are any secret passages, Miranda?' Jane tempted her.

'This is private property and we are guests,' Miranda replied.

'But you told me William Shakespeare wanted you to know all about the Playhouse. Don't you want to discover more about this place?'

'Yes, but in a manner that respects his trust. Also we should have Nathan as our guide.'

They were about to return to the party when William Shakespeare emerged with Peter from the main hall.

'There is much hidden within these walls and below where we stand now. For instance a tunnel leads to the old Gate-House, and there is a crypt and another special room,' William Shakespeare said to Miranda and Jane, pausing for a moment and then continuing.

'Nathan, one of my most trusted boy actors, will show you, as your uncle and I have other business to attend to. You will need to wear your cloaks, and can I suggest that you both use the hoods and put up your hair? There will be actors working below and we should not distract them!'

Nathan appeared in the doorway. Miranda could not hide her astonishment. Now no longer in costume, Nathan looked himself again. His portrayal of Prospero's daughter had completely disappeared from his face and his posture. She wondered how he was able to switch it on and off so quickly. Jane stared in fascination.

'Is anything the matter?' Nathan asked. Both girls, momentarily entranced by the loveliness of the boy's face, were unable to speak. Miranda was the first to remember her manners.

'We are delighted that you will be showing us the Playhouse, and possibly its secrets,' she replied.

'It is my pleasure. Wait here a moment.'

Nathan returned and opened a large, polished,

wooden door which led to a low candlelit hall with an arched ceiling. In the orange glow of the light Nathan's fine facial features were even more clearly defined. In these days when no women could act on the stage, it was essential that the audience fully believed in the boy actors when they played female roles. Their unbroken voices and the acting training they received meant that they were often mistaken for real girls.

Towards the end of the tunnel-like passage there was a Gothic arch that led down to the vaulted crypt of the old monastery. Although not owned by the King's Men, as the Playhouse was, the extra rooms were leased to provide vitally needed space.

Nathan carried a large candle and led the girls down the spiral stairs. At the bottom the light slowly penetrated the darkness and Miranda and Jane stared wide-eyed into the crypt.

'We are not quite there. Follow me through this next arch,' Nathan said.

'What's that?' Jane asked pointing to a heavy door.

'That is the entrance to a tunnel that leads to the Gate-House. There is a labyrinth of passageways hereabouts, some dating back to Roman times!'

In the half-light they could see a low-arched entrance and they could hear voices from within.

'Come in with me. But you must be very quiet!'

Towards the end of the tunnel-like passage there was a Gothic arch that led down to the vaulted crypt of the old monastery.

Nathan opened the door. At first the two girls could see very little, but as soon as they found their way into the low room, they froze in their tracks. In the centre of the room two boys of Nathan's age struggled for possession of a dagger that one held high above the head of the other. The atmosphere was alive with electricity while the boys battled. There was a group of about ten young actors seated at the far end of the room observing the fight, warming themselves by a log fire. The basement rooms were always cold, even in the spring and summer.

For some reason the room appeared to be far larger than it really was – being actually only forty feet long – and the boys by the fire seemed a long way away. An older man with bright ginger hair and a stern expression stood a few yards from the two boys locked in struggle. Miranda recognised him as the actor who had nearly expelled her from the stage, when she appeared from the chest during the rehearsal for *The Tempest*. The actor was clearly in control. One of the youths had a cruel and sinister look about him – his back bent and humped, as if he had a deformity. He was clearly the stronger as the fight reached its climax, and he started to overpower the other. The weaker youth fell – his own dagger wrestled from his hand. His opponent raised a long knife as if to strike the final deadly blow. Miranda nearly screamed out – but remembered that they had been told to be absolutely quiet when in the room.

Just at that point, the older man stepped forward with authority and clapped his hands loudly. Miranda and Jane nearly jumped out of their skins as the sound echoed around the stone walls of the room. The two young men in the fight released their grip upon each other and were immediately recognisable as young actors and not enemies in a fight. Mysteriously, the bent figure of the older boy righted itself as he regained his posture – it was as if the character had moulded his body only for the duration of the training and now that the playing was over he shook off the dark countenance of the king.

The two boys were released from the fighting position and seemed dazed, as if awakened from a trance. Both knives fell to the floor with a loud clatter and the older man placed them carefully into an open basket. Everyone stayed silent for a considerable time and the actor led the boys back to the group at the end of the room, praising them for doing so well.

'What is happening here?' Miranda asked Nathan.

'I have taken part in this sort of training and it is incredible to feel the tingles running up and down your spine as you act in this way. The murderous king Richard III is reserved for only the senior boys because he can be a risky character to play – he was an evil ruler. We came in at the climax as the boys were rehearsing a fight scene. One boy took the part of the king. Could you feel the menace in the room?'

Miranda and Jane nodded spellbound by the whole scene in front of them as Nathan continued.

'Richard III's wicked presence has been brought to life again. But this type of acting can only be practiced in controlled circumstances, otherwise a boy might be taken over by the role, and get wounded or worse! That was why the senior member of the troupe was watching everything so carefully. When fully trained, the boys will be able to deal with the intensity and be unaffected. It is a tremendous skill, which brings reality to the stage and William Shakespeare and the King's Men are masters of this art. One day when these boys reach the adult troupe they might actually play the characters in a production of the play, *Richard III*.

Most people think the boys are only trained to play female roles, but, as you can see, this is not the case. Many go on to act with the King's Men or at other theatres when their voices break.'

Miranda gazed in wonder at the now empty floor area, aware that there was much more to acting than she had realised. She looked again towards the boys at the far end of the room. Above them faintly glowing within the stone wall was the face of what looked like a king. It shimmered, silvery in hue. It disappeared as quickly as it had appeared.

'Did you see that?' she called out in wonder.

'What? Where?' Jane asked.

Miranda pointed. She saw the face momentarily reappear, but Jane could see nothing except the row of young actors. The image faded again.

Nathan indicated that it was time to leave.

'Did you see a face on the wall, Nathan?' Miranda asked.

'I think I did catch it out of the corner of my eye. But I am not certain what I saw exactly. William Shakespeare has told me such things can appear down here in the crypt. When he first made me aware of these faces

I wondered if this was the origin of the custom where we paint a portrait of a special person or family member and hang it in a room.'

'That is a really interesting idea,' Miranda said in response. Both girls looked hard again at the wall, but the face did not reappear.

Jane was first to leave the room. Miranda was about to follow when she heard her cousin cry out.

'Look, a figure! There's someone coming out of that wall!' Jane cried out pointing into the darkness of the crypt.

Nathan and Miranda were now standing beside her and, yes, there was a hazy white figure looming large in the dim light – seeming to appear out of nowhere. They stood transfixed until Nathan identified the spectre. It was William Shakespeare, still in his white monk's habit, accompanied by the girls' uncle!

'Where did you take Miranda and Jane, Nathan? These two young ladies look like they've seen a ghost!'

The Abbot's Study

Nathan led Miranda and Jane back upstairs.

'There is another room for you to see, but we must wait a while,' Nathan said.

'Could we go back to the main hall and talk a little?' Miranda asked.

'Yes – there is much to see there!' Nathan said, as he indicated that the two cousins follow him along a narrow pasageway.

Inside the grand chamber of the old monastery they wandered around looking up at the high-vaulted ceiling. Nathan pointed out the three levels of staging – with platforms above the main stage for special scenes to be enacted or for musicians to play from. He invited the girls to sit down on one of the pews that acted as seating for the public.

'Tell me about this place. Are there any real ghosts to see?' Miranda asked.

Nathan pointed out the three levels of staging – with platforms above the main stage for special scenes to be enacted or for the musicians to play from

'Every room and even this main hall has phantoms. Once, during a performance of *Hamlet* a real ghost was said to have appeared from out of the stone wall at the far end behind the stage. The spectre that floated into the theatre hall was so tormented that it was mistaken for the Prince's own murdered father and frightened the living daylights out of the audience!' Nathan was about to continue when an attendant called him.

'It is time we went to the study,' Nathan said, with an air of mystery.

The three left the main hall and Nathan led them to a corridor. 'This is a great privilege,' he said in a more serious tone as they arrived at a door. Nathan knocked and from within a voice invited them to enter.

'Welcome to my temporary work place!' William Shakespeare said. He stood by a large table, where their uncle also sat. 'This room was once the Abbot's study!'

It was surprisingly comfortable, given the cold stone walls of the ancient monastery. A large rug softened the harshness of the stone floor. The wood panelling gleamed and large volumes including a bible, and other religious and philosophical texts, were displayed on the bookshelf. Burning logs crackled comfortingly in the large fireplace, above which two griffins carved into the stonework stared fiercely into the room. Miranda and Jane stood motionless.

'*The Tempest* will be performed in November, but there are many preparations to make for our next production. Time waits for no man and our competitors are always hot on our heels!' William Shakespeare paused and then continued. 'I have matters to discuss with your uncle, but please look around the room and when we have finished I will answer any of your questions!'

Nathan stood vigilantly by the door as the two men sat together and spoke in hushed tones. The girls took the opportunity to investigate the study.

Jane was intrigued by an unusual drawing on one of the walls. It was a framed sketch that appeared to be of an imp standing on a stage amongst a group of actors. In the audience were people with their mouths wide open and horrified expressions on their faces. Miranda was curious about some of the paintings in the room. There were several small oil portraits and other pictures hanging on the walls and a plan drawing of the Globe Theatre in a gold frame. There was also a box containing some beautifully illustrated cards, which caught her attention.

Miranda walked towards one picture that intrigued her. It had a remarkable resemblance to William Shakespeare, but was clearly someone else – the gentleman's ruff and a fine silk shirt revealing he was a lord or knight. The more she studied the painting, the more she wondered if it was the face of the nobleman she had seen on the day she had observed the meetings from the props store.

'How curious,' she thought.

Miranda continued to explore the room and was drawn to a large book on one of the shelves. It contained amazingly detailed drawings and plans of ancient temples in Greece and Rome. As she glanced through the pages Miranda looked up and saw an engraving of a Greek goddess that for some reason she had not noticed until then. The figure stood tall and erect, wore an ornate helmet on her head and held a long spear. There was a snake at her feet, kept at bay by the goddess.

Miranda's focus on the engraving was interrupted as Nathan served biscuits and mead to everyone at William Shakespeare's request. The girls were then invited to ask the playwright about what they had seen.

'Sir, may I ask what that sketch represents?' Jane asked as she pointed at the framed picture of the sprite on stage at a performance, which had caught her attention when she had first looked around the room.

'Ah therein lies a tale,' Shakespeare replied. 'That was drawn by an artist who was in the audience of the play, *Dr Faustus*, written by one of my closest rivals – the eminent playwright Christopher Marlowe. It is not just a piece of entertainment but contains hidden magic. A serious actor or, better still, a mummer, worth his salt, can play the part so well that the spells begin to work, as if they were created by a real magician! On the particular occasion that inspired this picture, at the very climax of one of the spells, a thirteenth member of the twelve-man acting company appeared in their midst – quite literally out of nowhere. The mischievous imp, intent on naughtiness and monkey business, started to rise up above the stage and cackled so loudly that the audience fled from the theatre screaming!'

'Sir, can I ask why you are you so intrigued by such things?' Miranda asked boldly.

'Ever since I was a child I have been fascinated by drama and ghosts have always struck me as dramatic beings. They appear and disappear. They frighten us sometimes. They can even make noises and move things about!' Shakespeare paused for a moment. 'Ghosts and such like are for me a rather theatrical reminder that there is another world, not as familiar as this, which exists just around the corner. There is an unseen and mostly unknown world, which gives us those sensations that run up and down our spine or make things flash at the edge of our vision.'

'Like the shimmering face of a king I saw on the wall in the rehearsal room?'

'You saw such a manifestation?' the playwright asked, with immense interest.

Miranda recounted her experience and William Shakespeare listened intently. He was clearly impressed that she could perceive what was invisible to most people.

'Do you have another question?' William Shakespeare asked Jane.

'I love that drawing of the Globe Theatre,' Jane said, pointing at the architect's plan on the wall. She did not form a question but he responded nonetheless.

'Yes it is an accurate plan of the building. Would you like to know why there are the twelve signs of the zodiac on the ceiling above the stage and why it is called the Globe?'

Jane nodded, thrilled that he had taken up her enquiry.

'It was designed in a circle, but also as a globe – just as our own world is a round sphere with a firmament of stars above. Upon this stage we call Earth we are all players finding our part and acting out a story; some light and some dark; some serious and some amusing. My aim in writing the plays is not just to entertain, but to demonstrate these human roles through drama. The audience can then draw their conclusions as to the worthiness or otherwise of the actions people make – even characters from history!'

William Shakespeare paused for a moment, expecting another question.

'Sir, could you tell me the purpose for these picture cards? Are they a game?' Miranda asked, as she pointed towards a beautifully carved box.

'Those are not quite what they seem and can easily be mistaken for an amusement. A valued teacher who is now a close advisor to our troupe gave these specially illustrated cards to me many years ago, and they have been of immense value ever since in the playwriting. The pack is one of the Ferrara tarots and was designed over a hundred years ago. The first twenty-two cards are said to allow one to see into the future, and the others are for playing games. They are said to originate in ancient Egypt.'

'Sir, which stories or characters from your plays have they inspired?'

'There are many and it would need many hours to do them justice. For now, I will tell you about a few of them. The Magician, also known as the Juggler, is the first picture card in the pack. In my plays this is represented by the character Prospero. You know him well, having witnessed our writing of *The Tempest*. We each have this character within us, if we are wise and quiet enough to listen, and then bold enough to make the impossible achievable! Although this is shown as a man, a woman could equally play the role of Prospero one day in the future. When they are able to act on the stage, that is!'

Everyone in the room looked quite astonished at what he had said, but before anyone could speak, the playwright continued.

'Here is another and it is one of my favourites.'

He passed the card to Miranda and she studied the

fine illustration, edged with gold, of a painted chariot, driven by a noble king and pulled by a pair of fine white horses. William Shakespeare continued.

'Do you remember the rehearsals you observed at our Playhouse? They were for the play, *The Life of King Henry V*. This picture reminds me of the command

The picture was of a painted chariot, driven by a noble King
and pulled by a pair of fine white horses

Henry maintained as a general but also the compassion and self-control he showed as he took his men into battle.'

Miranda recalled the experience of being in the props store at the Playhouse and observing the playwright's face change as he acted as a mummer for the king, Henry V. It was that experience that had engraved forever in her mind that the King's Men were no ordinary acting troupe.

'One last question?'

'Sir, could I ask the name of the knight shown in the portrait and who is the Goddess in the engraving?'

Miranda asked, pointing at the small painting close to the book shelf and the picture hanging next to it.

'You ask two questions in one – but that is what I expect young people to do. You need to glean and gather all the knowledge you can from those who have it,' he said, pausing.

'Both pictures are very dear to me. The person in the painting is a knight whose name I cannot reveal. He is one of our patrons, but due to his high position he cannot publicly be seen to participate in our work or at our Playhouse. But he is a generous private contributor to our research and our plays, nonetheless. The engraving is of Pallas Athena, the Grecian goddess of wisdom.

'Sir, could I ask the name of the knight shown in the portrait
and who is the Goddess in the engraving?'

They both inspire my work, but it would take many
hours to explain why and now is not the time.'

'Thank you sir, you have been more than generous,'
Miranda said, sensing a profound seriousness in his
tone of voice. She wanted to show her appreciation for
the trouble he had taken with his answers, but sensed
that it was unnecessary.

'With your uncle's permission I would like Miranda

and Jane to observe some of the training that Nathan is being given here at the Playhouse. There has been an extraordinary step change in his development as an actor. Would you accompany them, Peter?'

'I will be pleased to,' he replied.

Miranda was obviously delighted, as it was not what she expected after William Shakespeare's reply regarding the pictures. She felt she had possibly gone too far with her questions.

With that the playwright left the study.

* * *

When they returned to the apothecary the girls were too excited to sleep and with a bowl of soup and freshly made bread to eat, they discussed the extraordinary party and the wonderful experience of witnessing the combat training and asking William Shakespeare questions in the Abbot's study. Miranda was thrilled that Jane was becoming as excited about the plays as she was, and when the food was all finished they went upstairs and sat on Miranda's bed. Gazing out of the window at the clear star-filled night, they could not wait to visit the Playhouse again.

A Special Training

During the following week, Peter suggested that Miranda learn more of the parts of Viola from William Shakespeare's play *Twelfth Night* and Rosalind from *As You Like It*. He said that they both contained wonderful lines for a young woman to act and whenever there was spare time he read for her and helped with the dramatisation of the roles. Jane meanwhile, decided to improve upon her dancing and playing of the lute. Although she enjoyed the theatre and meeting the boy players, she was not inclined to be an actor.

It was late afternoon on the day of Jupiter (Thursday), when Nathan brought a note, with a message inviting the two cousins, with their uncle, to the Playhouse again.

Miranda was always delighted to see Nathan, even if his visit by necessity was brief. As an apprentice to the actors he was needed for other duties at the theatre, in preparation for the evening ahead.

The girls had only a few hours to get ready, but were soon on their way along the lane towards Blackfriars with Peter. The sun was low on the horizon and in the sky above them the high wispy clouds were tinged with orange.

They arrived at the Playhouse and were taken to the theatre hall. Their entry was authorised solely by William Shakespeare, who had arranged with the training master that the three would be allowed to observe the tuition of the boy players. This was a very unusual request, but not questioned due to the authority and position of the playwright.

Nathan appeared at the door to the theatre and accompanied them to the first circle of seats, some twenty feet above the ground floor. There were two more galleries above them and it was the first time that Miranda had ever sat in this location in the Playhouse. All the hanging candles above the stage had been lit, but the rest of the hall was in darkness, creating an atmospheric setting. There was just enough light for her to marvel again at the size of the auditorium, which seemed even larger with all the seats unoccupied.

Nathan fetched drinks of mead and then excused himself as he was needed for preparations before the training. A little time later, assistants brought four large church candles in their holders onto the stage, placing one at each corner. When they were lit, the setting could easily have been mistaken for a magic show and this prompted Miranda to contemplate what Peter had said many times: that drama in its real sense was all about the supernatural.

The two cousins were immensely excited about what was about to take place on stage. A carved oak throne was placed on one side, and then draped with costumes and surrounded by props. There was a golden crown, several cloaks, some swords, a chalice, a box of rhinestone jewels, masks and other small objects not easy to identify. All was set and there was an intense silence in the auditorium.

The instructor entered and the boys were called out one by one. Each took his place next to his acting partner until there was a line of ten boys. Each pair of boys had prepared a scene from one of the plays regularly performed at the Playhouse, which they would be required to act out, whilst receiving coaching from the instructor.

A bell was rung to mark the start of the warm-ups. The boys were told to stand on the stage in a circle and, at the command of the instructor, two boys were selected at random to work together to improvise a dialogue with as much action as possible. Once it had been developed and each boy had contributed fully, the instructor called another boy's name to take over from one of those participating in the scene, and any acting stopped immediately. Miranda and Jane were struck by how the boys froze once their name was called. The slightest hint of a movement was resisted and the boys stood like statues until the scene restarted.

The bell sounded again and the next warm-up involved boys being called out individually to improvise using the props set out around the wooden throne. The instructor chose the item to be used and he helped the boys individually in adding more drama, or action, comedy, pathos or, if a female role was called for, the necessary femininity in speech and gesture. Nathan's partner in the exercise was a boy called John. He was taller than Nathan and was chosen to act the role of a wicked Queen, plotting the death of her husband. His characterisation was so realistic that the girls became quite frightened by the malevolent countenance he generated through his acting. It reminded Miranda of the play *Hamlet* that she had been given by William Shakespeare and read aloud to Jane.

Now the boys were suitably warmed up, the instructor asked them to be seated in front of the stage. He then introduced the main work of the session, which he described as a method of acting used by the King's Men to transform and take a play from the page upon which it was written onto the stage in front of an audience. He explained that because the playwright created stories and dialogue and action from his inner imagination, the actor must know how to make those imaginary circumstances real to himself first, rather than to play to the the audience alone. Each pair of boys had worked on a scene that they had prepared. Nathan and John were selected first. Theirs was from the play called *Cymbeline*, which had been performed by the King's Men only a few months before at the Playhouse.

The two boys played Imogen's two long lost brothers, Guiderius and Arviragus, in the scene where they are laying the evil stepson of King Cymbeline to rest after he has been slain and beheaded. They performed an impromptu but reverent funeral ceremony, by singing a song for his passing, for although the son of the King had become their enemy, he was due a prince's burial. The instructor set the scene in the deepest of winter, and wanted the boys to behave as if a cruel wind was cutting through their garments, chilling their bodies as they sung and performed the lines.

'Act as if this is really happening to you!' the instructor exhorted the two boys, as they began to recreate the feelings of intense cold weather in themselves. Nathan's face contorted as he acted the painful sensation of his nose and ears starting to freeze. John moved to protect his body from the elements by turning against the imaginary blasts of cold air and then he, too, became pale – his hands and feet growing numb.

Miranda and Jane looked on in wonder. It was a warm summer evening and they thought the exercise most difficult for the boys.

When the instructor was satisfied that they had sufficiently recreated the sensations in themselves he made a command to the musicians. The two viol players started slowly with a sombre piece of music and the flute joined in with a quietly haunting tone, evoking a winter setting. The drum created a suitably solemn beat as Nathan and John stood still within the area marked out with the large candles. A third boy lay as dead, playing the beheaded prince.

Closely watched by the instructor, the two boys began to sing the most evocative of funeral songs. Miranda and Jane were impressed that the boys not only acted to an exceptionally high standard, but sang excellently as well. The prose selected was rarely performed as a song by the adult troupe and so the boys' rendition of the homily was very moving. Commanded that they still maintain the portrayal of this happening in a wild exposed place in the freezing cold, the scene was acted out with absolute seriousness and the auditorium was hushed in silence. The only sound, apart from the boys singing, was that of musicians playing their accompaniment.

Nathan (as Guiderius) started to sing:
Fear no more the heat o' th' sun,
Nor the furious winter's rages,
Thou thy worldly task hast done,
Home art gone, and ta'en thy wages.

Golden lads and girls all must,
As chimney-sweepers, come to dust.
John next sings, playing the part of Arviragus:
Fear no more the frown o' th' great,
Thou art past the tyrant's stroke,
Care no more to clothe and eat,
To thee the reed is as the oak:
The sceptre, learning, physic, must
All follow this and come to dust.
Guiderius:
Fear no more the lightning-flash.
Arviragus:
Nor th' all-dreaded thunder-stone.
Guiderius:
Fear not slander, censure rash.
Arviragus:
Thou hast finish'd joy and moan.
Then Guiderius and Arviragus sing together:
All lovers young, all lovers must
Consign to thee and come to dust.

Due to time constraints, the instructor asked the two boy players to stop and come out of role. The musicians also ceased playing and the whole auditorium was completely silent. Miranda and Jane sat as close to each other as they could – very much in awe of the scene that had just been acted on stage. They particularly appreciated the wonderful beauty and depth in the song – each part containing so many wisdoms. They were also impressed by the excellent portrayal of the two brothers by Nathan and John.

The boys were now in a huddled conversation with the instructor and this went on for some time. Eventually, they were sent back to their seats in front of the stage. From the look on their faces, the instructor was clearly pleased with their performance.

A break was announced, but before the boys were released they all formed a line. The bell was rung for a final time and the musicians started to play what seemed to be a pre-arranged melody. The notes from the flute were as light as a butterfly in flight and were high, without being shrill, and the playing of the lute and drum added to a sense of inner happiness. While the music continued, each boy player began to quietly call over to himself some sort of prayer, all with their heads slightly bowed.

Miranda was intrigued. 'What are they saying to themselves?' she wondered, determined to ask Nathan when she next spoke to him.

After a little while, once every boy had finished, they broke from the line and went for some well-earned mead and cake.

Nathan and John both came up to the gallery bringing with them some of the refreshments. The two boys told Miranda and Jane and their uncle that the training would be going on late into the night and it was best that they leave before the next part began. The two cousins looked terribly disappointed, but they could see the sense in the decision.

Uncle Peter walked with Jane and John back to the main auditorium, leaving Miranda and Nathan alone.

'It was a wonderful experience to be able to observe you in training,' Miranda said.

'I am glad you found it interesting. My nerves were jumping all over the place. You can't believe how intense it is on stage.'

'Before we must leave, can I ask what prayer you were calling over to yourself at the end of the training session?'

'I don't think it's a secret,' he said with a smile, before continuing.

'William Shakespeare has said many times that we need to call over our hope and desire to become the finest of players and to one day be accepted as an apprentice to the senior troupe. We imagine ourselves in the future fulfilling what we aim to be. In essence, we become what we often think about and Mr. Shakespeare has said many times 'attract your future by dwelling on it constantly'. I believe that as we learn more and develop our arts and skills, we will create the future that we want for ourselves. It was this secret that was the key to William Shakespeare's own personal transformation from a lowly grammar school boy in Stratford-upon-Avon to becoming the most influential playwright in London and a member of the King's Men.'

Miranda looked intrigued and fascinated. 'Thank you, Nathan. Another day I would like to ask you more about your training.'

'I am sure you can, but I had better get back now!'

* * *

A few weeks later Miranda sat alone in her room overlooking the City. Jane had returned to Rochester, the plague having abated there. They both hoped they would be together again soon, but that was in the hands of the adults.

Summer was the busiest season for the theatres of London and Miranda accepted that it was very unlikely that she would see much of Nathan. The performances of William Shakespeare's plays *The Winter's Tale*, *Macbeth* and *Cymbeline*, at the Playhouse and the rehearsals for his new play, *The Tempest*, kept every actor, apprentice and senior member of the troupe busy. To add to his workload Nathan was engrossed in learning the role of Miranda. He kindly commented several times that his task was made much lighter through his acquaintance with the real Miranda, and this pleased her very much.

Autumn's leaves had fallen and cold winter winds arrived in the City before Miranda would learn more of the secrets of the King's Men.

Part Three

Christmastide 1611

In the Library

It was a gloriously bright but freezing December morning in 1611. Near to an area close to the City of London known as High Holborn, a grand house stood proudly in its own grounds. Two people wearing long winter coats, a middle-aged man and a teenage girl, looked up at the leaded windows of the upper storeys sparkling in the winter sunshine.

The man knocked on the door. It was opened ceremoniously. Peter handed his niece's music case to a male attendant, who nodded without speaking. Smiling at Miranda, her uncle left to return to the apothecary, knowing she was in safe hands. She walked into the warm but dimly-lit hallway of the house and waited patiently. A plentiful pile of logs crackled in the large grate creating a welcoming orange glow and above the fireplace an imposing portrait of a regal-looking duchess seemed to stare at her in silence. She resisted the temptation to go over and warm her hands by the fire.

Above the fireplace an imposing portrait of a regal-looking duchess
seemed to stare at her in silence

Christmas was approaching and it was the time for the rich to eat, drink and be merry, to prepare themselves for the cold, dark months of January and February. The twelve days of Christmastide, beginning on Christmas Day, were one of the highlights of the year for the wealthy owners of the grand house – with feasting, parties and performances by theatre troupes. They were rich enough to employ a group of boys to perform a shortened adaptation of the play *Twelfth Night*. The King's Men originally produced the play for Queen Elizabeth, although there was talk that William Shakespeare had originally written it with a boys' company in mind.

The attendant carried Miranda's instrument case and led her up the stairs. She tried to study the paintings that lined the staircase as best she could in the dull light, but she passed them too quickly to appreciate them. When they reached the upper landing the attendant bowed and she was shown into the room where she would be working. It was an exquisite library.

After the gloom of the hall, the shafts of bright winter sunshine streaming through the narrow, arched windows that lined the long room filled her with delight. The door closed leaving her alone. She stared around her. Besides the well-stocked bookshelves, there were several tables and chairs and also musical instruments. She presumed they were set up ready for a group to play, to entertain the gentlemen and ladies over Christmas.

Breathing in the atmosphere of the room Miranda felt as if she was inhaling the knowledge that emanated from the rows of thick volumes on the shelves. She studied the titles on the spines of the books displayed closest to her. She saw a copy of *The Lives of the Noble Grecians and Romans* by Plutarch that she knew had been used by William Shakespeare for plays such as *Julius Caesar* and *Titus Andronicus*. This was a source of reference for historical accuracy and given the broad range of other subjects displayed on the shelves, she was sure the library would have provided exceptional information for the playwright. The value of the books was incalculable, given the scarcity and cost of printed material.

Taking a seat by the instruments, Miranda recalled her task today. It involved her playing music but, beyond that, the detail was hazy. She opened her old battered instrument case with some nervousness.

She heard voices on the stairs and wondered if they were musicians, but the two gentlemen ushered in by the attendant looked far too bookish and stern. They politely acknowledged her and then purposefully positioned paper, ink wells and quills on the very large walnut table in the centre of the room. The two men settled down and waited quietly.

There were more voices in the hall. The door to the library opened and William Shakespeare entered, accompanied by Nathan. The playwright's presence seemed more commanding than when Miranda had seen him last. The very successful first performance of his play *The Tempest* in front of King James, a little over a month before, had set the Royal Court buzzing. The enormous impact of the play's philosophical content and its use of music, masque and overall entertainment value had left Shakespeare's royal patron eager for even greater things. Nathan's personal charisma was likewise enhanced and his career with the senior troupe was assured following his successful performance in the role of Prospero's daughter.

Miranda turned and her face immediately lit up when she saw Nathan. His face was, as required for the stage, beardless, fresh-complexioned and youthful. She was thrilled to be in the same room as he was becoming quite a star, but she also hoped that this new-found fame would not lessen his affection for her. He beamed when he saw her and she relaxed. He did not approach her as there was work to be accomplished, but a friendly wink from him assured Miranda that all was well.

She knew that Nathan would continue as a boy player until his voice broke. His next commitment was as Viola in *Twelfth Night*, scheduled for several performances over Christmas, including the one at this very house. If the convention of the day had allowed, Miranda would have really enjoyed performing the part of Viola on stage. The comic use of disguises in the play is much developed by William Shakespeare and she had studied fragments of the script many times in her uncle's collection of books. She giggled to herself as she remembered some of the interrelationships in the plot.

Viola is a girl who has been shipwrecked with her twin brother on a remote island. Separated from him and to survive unchaperoned and without a protector, she disguises herself as a boy called Cesario and finds employment with the Duke Orsino, who is in love with a beautiful lady called Olivia. The Duke uses Viola, now disguised as Cesario, to act as his go-between, as he is attempting to woo Olivia. Viola realises she is in a difficult position when Olivia seems more romantically interested in Cesario than the Duke Orsino. Miranda imagined the island where Viola's strange predicament is played out.

'You look miles away, Miranda!' The gentle, but firm voice of William Shakespeare brought her back to the present.

'I apologise, Sir.'

'No need. I see you are set up to play your lute. I am sure you will find this an interesting experience and I will thank your uncle again for giving his permission for you to help us today. Your sentiment towards our work, rather than your playing, is why you have been chosen. So do relax. Nathan will give you instructions shortly.'

She smiled and waited patiently. After a little while, Nathan came and stood next to her. His closeness made her blush slightly. She selected a piece of lute music by John Dowland, and waited patiently to begin playing.

William Shakespeare went over to the two scribes at the table and shook their hands politely as they both rose from their seats.

'So, it is time to begin!' he said to them.

The playwright had used scribes ever since his eyesight became too poor for his work. Many years of writing and reading by candlelight had taken their toll.

Nathan indicated that Miranda should start to play her first piece. The atmosphere settled. Besides the music all that could be heard were the voices of William Shakespeare and the scribes. Nathan's mind wandered a little as the writing began. He longed to immerse himself in the script he was learning – urgently needing to refresh the lines for the role of Viola. However, he knew this would be a distraction for the playwright.

Miranda continued until William Shakespeare turned and looked in Nathan's direction. Nathan refocused and with a lowered voice told Miranda that he was going to help her play in a way that would be as conducive as possible to the writing. He explained that the playwright was working on an entirely new play with John Fletcher, a co-writer for the King's Men. Called *All Is True* it tells the story of the power struggle in the Tudor Court between nobles and the ambitious Cardinal Wolsey, the King's first minister. There is a great deal of music in the play, which Nathan thought Miranda would be interested in. Its other title was *The Life of King Henry VIII*.

Nathan, in his usual friendly way, made clear to her that he was to help her find a rhythm that was harmonious with the beat of five, known as iambic pentameter. This she knew from her Greek studies was the style of poetry that William Shakespeare used in his plays.

The metre in the verse is a recurring pattern of stressed and unstressed syllables in lines of a set length of five pairs – quite natural to the English language. Miranda recalled how her uncle quoted one of his favourite lines of William Shakespeare's poetry. He emphasised the stressed parts and spoke more quietly the unstressed parts: 'Shall **I** compare thee **to** a **summer's day**?' He would say the line from the sonnet in a most dramatic way, whilst Miranda laughed.

Asking Miranda's permission, Nathan lifted her left hand gently and placed the first and second two fingers on the inside of her right wrist – at the pulse. Once she got over the thrill of him holding her hand she relaxed and soon felt the beat of her own pulse. Her mind started to fill with an intense excitement that it was her own heart she was feeling and she then realised that the speed of writing used by the playwright – five beats to a line of speech, synchronised with the same rhythm. Her fingers went back to playing the lute and closing her eyes she felt her own heart beat slow down as she harmonised with the writing. Her playing settled and subtly changed. William Shakespeare did not respond with any outward display, but he appeared pleased and relaxed. Rising from his chair he went across to the bookshelves and, after selecting a particular volume, opened the large leather bound book. He appeared to know the text well and began to dictate to the scribes.

Within a short while, they were writing at a fantastic pace, as if connected to a generator in the poet's mind. After nearly an hour of continuous writing, William Shakespeare asked Nathan to fetch refreshments. He brought in sweet mead made with honey and thick oat biscuits. They were set out on a table and everyone helped themselves.

'Well done for your playing today, Miranda,' William Shakespeare praised her. 'You are clearly very receptive to new ideas and that is to your credit. Please look at this section of the play that was started by my colleague John Fletcher, which I have added to today. I think with music it will work very well. It is a little of the bard in me,' he added with a look of wisdom upon his face.

Responding to his instruction, one of the scribes passed a piece of paper to Miranda on which two verses of a song had been written.

She could smell the fresh ink as she read the lines:

Orpheus with his lute made trees,
And the mountain tops that freeze,
Bow themselves when he did sing:
To his music plants and flowers
Ever sprung, as sun and showers
There had made a lasting spring.

Every thing that heard him play,
Even the billows of the sea,
Hung their heads and then lay by:
In sweet music is such art,
Killing care and grief of heart
Fall asleep, or hearing die.

'I hope I can hear it one day, when it is played,' Miranda said.

'It will be completed quite soon I hope, although I feel it needs a further verse,' Shakespeare replied.

A male attendant entered and spoke to the playwright

and Miranda heard voices in the hallway below and footsteps approaching the room. William Shakespeare's momentary relaxation suddenly came to an end.

It was announced that the work of the day was to finish as a visitor was arriving within minutes to collect William Shakespeare for a special meeting. Books and papers were hurriedly gathered up and the playwright, accompanied by the scribes, left the library. Nathan was instructed to take Miranda to the Blackfriars Playhouse once he had attended to William Shakespeare.

'There are no plays being performed today and I have been given permission to show you any parts of the theatre you have not yet seen. I will then escort you to the apothecary,' he said as he left the room.

Now alone in the library Miranda collected up her music and packed away the lute. She noticed a small

Miranda could clearly see that one A was shown in white
and the other A was shaded.

book had been left on the scribes' table. Nathan was downstairs attending to William Shakespeare and she was tempted to open it and look inside. She wondered if it might be a play that she had not seen.

On the first page of the book was an ornately decorated engraving of a double A A symbol. Miranda could clearly see that one A was shown in white and the other A was shaded.

Looking further through the book she was delighted to discover that it was a copy of the play *The Tempest* and she was thrilled to see in the cast list the character Miranda as Prospero's daughter. She could not resist reading further.

She was immediately intrigued that the first letters of the two words in the title were underlined, with the number 33 scribbled below.

The Tempest

33

Miranda had no idea why the number had been scribbled there and what on earth it had to do with the title. 'Was it the playwright's thirty-third play?'

She searched further through the book and in Act 1, Scene 2, she discovered a name had been written by hand alongside the text where the Miranda in the play speaks to her father and the first letter of the second and third line and the first three letters of the fourth line had been made bold and underlined using an ink quill.

Miranda speaks to Prospero, her father:
You have often
__Be__gun to tell me what I am, but stopped
__A__nd left me to a bootless inquisition,   *Franciſ*
__Con__cluding, 'Stay, not yet'.

The letters clearly spelt the word B-A-Con in the text and 'Francis' was scribbled by hand in the margin.

'Sir Francis Bacon? Why would his name be shown here?'

She recalled how William Shakespeare had declined to identify the knight shown in one of the portraits in the Abbot's study at the Playhouse. She was convinced this was the same man and was the gentleman who had met with the playwright on the day she observed the play writing from the props store. He was a very important figure at the Royal Court and was an historian, poet and philosopher, and chief editor of the new Bible, just completed for King James. However she had no idea why someone had purposefully set the name within the text – even if in a concealed way. She studied the page of script again and again and the lines that the character Miranda speaks seemed to indicate that some hitherto unknown truth was being revealed.

Still intrigued she decided to look further through the play. There were no other obvious margin notes and she had nearly closed the book when she decided to look at the final page. She was thrilled to see that FRANCIS and 33 had both been scribbled in the margin and the final word of the epilogue spoken by Prospero was highlighted. Miranda had no idea what significance this might have. She read Prospero's epilogue and spoke out loud the last few lines to herself, wondering if they had a particular meaning and why the word 'free' had been highlighted in the text:

As you from crimes would pardoned be,
Let your indulgence set me **free**.

33
Francis

135

Although tempted to search for more scribbled notes in the text, Miranda was worried she was getting drawn into something that was none of her business. She closed the book and placed it back onto the table.

Just at that moment, there were footsteps in the hall and Nathan re-entered the library. They went down the stairs and left the house, heading back towards the City.

On the way Miranda could not help wondering if the copy of the play *The Tempest* she had found in the library belonged to William Shakespeare or had been left by someone else. Whoever the owner, she was intrigued to know what significance, if any, the names and numbers scribbled in the play might have.

A Person of Letters

Leaving High Holborn a steep path winds its way down towards the City. Nathan, with Miranda at his side, stopped to admire the view as the bright sunshine was just beginning to melt the ice on the steps. Preparing to start the descent, she smiled as he offered to hold her instrument case.

'This place reminds me of something I learnt at training the other day. Our instructor told us that it was often a test of a young bard to wait overnight alone in a high place, such as a snow-covered mountain crag. In the morning he was tested by the elders and he would need to be able to create verse there and then on any subject decided by them,' Nathan said.

'Do you think William Shakespeare at an earlier stage in his life, faced challenges to achieve his mastery of poetry and play writing?' Miranda asked, as they carefully made their way down the steps.

'I have managed to glean the odd gem from time to time,' Nathan replied, walking one step in front to make sure she could not fall. 'I know that when William Shakespeare first came to London as an unknown poet, his talent was soon recognised by some very important people. He was tutored in knowledge hard to access for most and given permission to use books on a multitude of subjects available only to the privileged few. This was how he was introduced to the hidden power and meaning of the English language and subjects such as philosophy. For many years he struggled to develop his skills and achieved a personal transformation, taking him from a lowly grammar-school-educated poet to a respected actor and playwright. His skill was recognised and he was elevated to the Queen's own theatre company known as the Lord Chamberlain's Men and then finally became the principal writer for the productions by the King's own troupe.'

'That makes some sense of that wonderful library at the house,' said Miranda.

'These King's Men players are much more than they seem – I call them *magicians* myself. That Playhouse of theirs is full of interesting stuff and my friends and I, the boy players, get to do all sorts of amazing acting – such as the exercises you watched during our training over the summer.'

Miranda found the descent a little difficult and Nathan took her hand – not wanting her to slip. She thanked him and beamed with pleasure, comforted by his touch and happy that they were getting closer to one another all the time.

At the bottom of the hill they made their way through the labyrinth of narrow lanes towards the City. They turned a corner and could see the dark monastery at Blackfriars ahead.

Walking through the small cemetery, Nathan opened the side entrance that was sometimes used as a stage door. The old hinges creaked loudly and Miranda recalled her own escapade when she first visited the props store above the tiring house. Inside, the old stone steps that led steeply up to the first floor were as dark as she remembered. Nathan lit a small candle to give better light and they soon found themselves close to the central stage area inside the grand meeting chamber of the Playhouse. It was very cold, so Nathan fetched Miranda a warmer coat.

Taking any opportunity to act she stood on the stage and closed her eyes, imagining the auditorium full of

Walking through the small cemetery, Nathan opened the side entrance that was sometimes used as a stage door.

people. Nathan took a seat on the front row bench and clapped his hands loudly, cheering and whistling.

Miranda was a little nervous performing in front of her now famous boy player friend but she settled herself and began to recite lines from the play *Twelfth Night* spoken by the heroine Viola. She knew the verse well, having been helped to learn her favourite scenes by her uncle.

She spoke each line with passion and feeling:

> *Make me a willow cabin at your gate,*
> *And call upon my soul within the house;*
> *Write loyal cantons of contemned love,*
> *And sing them loud even in the dead of night;*
> *Halloo your name to the reverberate hills,*
> *And make the babbling gossip of the air*
> *Cry out 'Olivia!' O, you should not rest*
> *Between the elements of air and earth,*
> *But you should pity me.*

'Fantastic! You are wonderful and that could have been me on stage!' Nathan shouted up from the bench – surprised that she knew and acted the lines so confidently.

Miranda bowed and took Nathan's applause and compliment.

'I know it could never be possible, but we would make a great partnership for the play! I could be Viola and you the Duke Orsino,' she said, coming down from the stage.

Nathan was not sure what to say. He looked a little uncomfortable. He had never contemplated acting on stage with a girl.

'Don't worry Nathan; I am sure it will never happen!' Miranda added, seeing his discomfort. 'Can I tell you something in confidence?'

'Of course you can, but let us look for somewhere warm so that we can concentrate.'

They found a small room used by the boy players, and Nathan lit the fire and brought mead from the kitchen.

'I get the sense you have something very interesting to let me in on!' Nathan said with a cheeky grin.

'Just before we left the library at the big house, I found a copy of *The Tempest* on the table used by the scribes. I couldn't resist opening it, as it has only just been performed for the first time and I was intrigued to see some of the lines you must have had to learn to play the character, Miranda.'

'It was probably the hardest role I have ever performed and it was nerve-racking to play in front of King James at the Royal Court. Whenever I doubted myself, I thought of all my training and then pictured your face in my mind – the real Miranda in my life.'

'Nathan, you say such wonderful things,' she said, blushing and not knowing what to say. It was the first time in her life anyone outside of her family had expressed such value for her.

'I am sorry if I have embarrassed you.'

'It is the nicest thing that has ever been said to me,' she added, with a slight sob.

'Well, ever since you appeared as if by magic on the stage during the rehearsals for the play you have been the *real* Miranda for me,' he said, putting his arm around her in a comforting way until a smile returned to her face. 'Come on, tell me all about what you discovered in the copy of the play. What was it that so interested you?'

Miranda composed herself and then continued, warmed by Nathan's closeness to her.

'There were strange notes scribbled alongside the script – numbers and names written by hand in very specific parts of the text.'

'I know that many of the published plays have little secrets hidden in the text – the clever people call them acrostic messages and ciphers. An example would be a name concealed within a sentence or a section of speech. Symbols, numbers and engravings can all mean something. What did you find, exactly?'

Miranda fetched a piece of rough paper and using a quill and ink drew out what she had found in the book. She described it all as she re-created the text.

'The title page clearly had an engraving of a double A A – as if this was a symbol of the publisher or author. Next, when I found the play text, there was the number 33 scribbled beneath the title *The Tempest* and the first T in each word underlined. I presumed they were some sort of editorial comments, but I found the same number and a name next to certain lines in the text.'

'Bless me – that is really interesting! What message did you find?'

She wrote down the lines exactly as she remembered them from Act I showing how the word B-A-Con was highlighted in the text, with the name FRANCIS written in the margin.

'Did its place in the text seem significant?' Nathan asked as he studied the four lines spoken by Miranda in the play.

'I am not sure. It starts where Miranda says to Prospero: *Begun to tell me what I am, but stopped.*'

'I know that part well, let me continue: *And left me to a bootless inquisition. Concluding, 'Stay, not yet.'* I had no idea the words contained the hidden name of Sir Francis Bacon. Where is it shown again?'

'The B and A of the first two lines and the three letters of the third line CON were bold and underlined.'

'You have probably already worked out that the person shown is Sir Francis Bacon, but I am not sure yet what the 33 means. Will you let me be a bit intellectual for a moment?'

'I would love that!'

'William Shakespeare, as well as being a bard and playwright can be called *A Person of Letters*. Let me explain.'

She nodded, pleased that he had taken her discovery in the library so seriously.

'When it is said about someone 'He is a person of letters', this can have a meaning at all sorts of levels.

Firstly, it can indicate someone who can read and write and have knowledge of, and can use the letters of, a language such as English or Latin. The next step up is that there are people who have earned letters before or after their name – such as a degree, a doctorate, a knight, a nobleman, a lord or learned man. These people may have written books, poetry and works with a deeper meaning and significance. A good example is Christopher Marlowe, who gained his degree at Cambridge and went on to author plays that have often been compared with William Shakespeare's in their importance. Can you see where this is going?' He paused.

'Yes. What's the next level?' Miranda asked, eager for him to continue.

'This is where a person understands the hidden meaning of letters and the power of the alphabet, root numbers, ciphers and the evolution of language. A *Person of Letters* took William Shakespeare under his wing when the playwright first came to London to begin his career. His name is Sir Francis Bacon. With his help, philosophical and esoteric understandings were included in the plays and the vocabulary expanded to include many, many new words, which are now becoming embedded in the English language.'

'Goodness. Why would he want to remain so anonymous?'

'Playwrights, players and us boy players are not well respected by higher society and that is a polite way of putting it! No lord or sir is going to openly admit a partnership with William Shakespeare, even if they personally recognise his genius or the significance of his writing and poetry.'

'Why use *The Tempest* to convey this hidden clue to Bacon's identity?'

'It is probably the play that best conveys the beliefs of the King's Men. It is no doubt one of William Shakespeare's most philosophical writings. I bet 33 is a cipher number.'

'What do you mean?'

'This is another thing I gleaned – how to work out the number associated with a word. I will show you.'

Nathan withdrew his arm from around Miranda and picked up the same piece of paper. Using a quill he carefully wrote out the 24 letters of their alphabet with a number shown below each one.

A	B	C	D	E	F	G	H	I/J	K	L	M
1	2	3	4	5	6	7	8	9	10	11	12

N	O	P	Q	R	S	T	U/V	W	X	Y	Z
13	14	15	16	17	18	19	20	21	22	23	24

'I bet the word FRANCIS or BACON can be linked to the number shown in the text.'

By adding up the numbers associated with each letter he quickly discovered that the letters in the acrostic B-A-Con added up to thirty-three.

'Yes – what did I tell you? That was a bit of luck, though. I'll keep working on the other things you have shown me and possibly your uncle can help as well.'

'I will ask him as soon as I can.'

'Come, let's explore the Playhouse!' Nathan said leading Miranda to a corridor, beyond a small kitchen. It was so dark that he had to fetch a candle to illuminate a steep spiral staircase.

'This will be your first experience as a bard in training!' he said, with a cheeky grin.

The Spear Shaker

The stone stairway behind the stage at the Playhouse was extremely narrow and confined. At each level there was a small window through which Miranda could see the alley below and the people passing looked tiny. They eventually reached the highest platform where their heads were almost touching the high ceiling of the monastery.

A closed door beckoned ahead. Getting down on his knees Nathan stretched forward and turned a large brass handle. The door creaked open and Miranda muffled a scream as a large rat scurried across the floor. Bravely, she edged forward.

A small window at the far end meant there was just enough light for her to see inside the room and in the

The stone stairway behind the stage at the Playhouse
was extremely narrow and confined.

gloom, it appeared to be a very small attic space with
a low wooden ceiling. There was a raised open box of
wood in the centre and, above, was a pulley and ropes.
Miranda started to step over the boards of the box, but
gasped as she felt a sudden rush of vertigo. She could
see down to the stage below.

'Are you all right, Miranda?' Nathan asked as he caught up behind her. They were both crouched in the roof space.

'I am fine, I think. I looked through the trapdoor and realised how high we were. It scared me!'

'Now you might have some sympathy for me being stuck up here for hours and hours on end!' Nathan said.

She didn't understand what he meant, but in the gloom she felt the presence of some objects that she could not see. She was glad he was with her.

Nathan brought in the candle and Miranda nearly jumped out of her skin. Ahead was a huge shining gold painted eagle with wings outstretched. Its jewelled eyes flashed. Since her experience in the props store she was accustomed to the odd and curious objects owned by the King's Men, but this creature unnerved her. The next prop was a large crescent moon painted silver and, on the floor, other properties not so easy to identify.

'Where are we?' she asked.

'This is an enclosure known as The Heavens because it is suspended from the highest point of the vaulted ceiling. Props, or even actors, can be lowered from here onto the stage for the productions. I wanted you to experience what I have felt, perched here high above the stage waiting for the right moment in the play to send a silver moon or gold eagle down using the rope pulley. This is your first test as a young bard in training.'

She smiled at him pleased at how courageous she felt high above the stage.

They were just about to go back down to the ground floor when Nathan spotted two people come onto the stage below. Putting his finger to his lips he indicated that she should not speak. It was not that they were in The Heavens without permission but more that they should not interrupt any meeting taking place between such important people.

She took another look down through the gap in the trapdoor and was unable to contain her surprise. There below was the man she had observed from the props store in February – his position at Court clearly shown by his fancy ruff, silk jacket, hat and distinctive beard. He was in close conversation with William Shakespeare and as she had commented before, their features were very similar. If it had not been for their difference in rank and station identified by their clothes and the rich jewels worn by the knight, she would have thought they were brothers.

'I can't believe it, that is Sir Francis Bacon below us with Mr. Shakespeare,' Nathan said.

Miranda nodded spellbound by the two men walking and talking below them.

Just at that moment Sir Francis Bacon looked up towards The Heavens where Miranda and Nathan crouched uncomfortably. They both froze. The next few minutes seemed to last an eternity, but very soon he returned to speaking to the playwright – it was as if they were discussing a production of a play. After some more conversation they left the stage. A door banged shut.

'This was clearly a private meeting. They have gone down to the crypt, rather than use the main door. There is a little used passageway that leads to the Blackfriars Gate-House,' Nathan said.

Miranda and Nathan both stared at each other, amazed that the gentleman whose identity they had only just been discussing in relation to the play *The Tempest*, should unexpectedly appear at the Playhouse.

'Maybe they are collaborating in some way?' Nathan suggested.

'Possibly this was the reason why William Shakespeare

had to leave the play-writing so urgently at the grand house near High Holborn.'

Nathan carefully led Miranda out of the tight space and back onto the stairway.

They made their way down the steep steps to the theatre hall.

'I must go and tidy up the study in case they have left any plates or tankards to be put away. Please wait here a moment,' Nathan said.

Miranda sat by the stage and mused on her wonderful experience assisting in the library. 'I can't believe how lucky I am!' she thought.

'You'll never guess what I found?' Nathan said as he reappeared a few minutes later balancing several empty flagons in his hands, trying not to drop them on the stone floor.

'Did you find more hidden names and numbers?'

'No. But I think have discovered the meaning of the double A A symbol. I am sure that the engraving you saw in the copy of *The Tempest* is laid out on the desk in the study. It is exactly as you described it with one A in white and one shaded A. It looks like it is being prepared for a book and has been designed carefully with the words 'In Honour of the Muse Athena – the Spear Shaker' written in beautiful script. Beneath the engraving is the Goddess's picture – you know, the same one that hangs on the wall by the bookshelf.'

'The 'Spear Shaker' – but that is William Shakespeare's surname rearranged, isn't it? How could his name possibly be relevant to a goddess from Greece?' Miranda asked.

'I am not sure, but it suggests that the A in the engraving represents the goddess Athena and for whatever reason this is important,' Nathan replied.

'Is Spear Shaker another name of the Goddess Athena?'

'I am not sure, but your uncle would know,' Nathan replied.

'What an amazing day. We have so much to learn!' Miranda added.

'Let's get back to the apothecary!' Nathan said, after returning from the kitchen. They made their way to the ground floor and taking a large key from his pocket he secured the side door as they left.

Welcoming lights glowed in the study as they arrived and, through a window, they could see Uncle Peter sitting at his desk.

'Good night, Nathan!' she said warmly, aware how much she had enjoyed the time at the Playhouse and, in particular, their conversation about the cryptic messages in the plays.

'When William Shakespeare said I could show you more of the secrets of the Blackfriars I am not sure he meant for you to see quite as much as you have today!' he chuckled. He then walked back down the lane.

Miranda made her way up to her room and sat on her bed, a little dazed after the visit to the Playhouse. She rested back onto a large cushion and slept.

Later, Peter came up to her room.

'Are you well?' he asked.

'Yes, Uncle, I am. I was just daydreaming!'

'I have news for you about your Christmas at home in St. Albans. Your father wants you to return here to the apothecary for Twelfth Night as he needs to attend to a private matter.'

Although Miranda was thrilled that she would be returning so soon, she thought sadly about her mother. This was the second Christmas they had not all been together as a family and nothing had been the same since her sudden death from a fever.

'Your father understands that you should not be too alone at the end of Christmastide and has arranged for your cousin Jane to visit as well.'

'What a wonderful Twelfth Night is in store for us all!' Miranda said, with delight in her voice.

Peter suggested that she come downstairs to his study and asked Cathy to make mead for them both. Placing a log on the fire he resolved to change the subject of conversation away from family issues.

'How was your time at the grand house near High Holborn?'

Miranda's day had been so full of amazing things that she had almost forgotten her morning in the library. She told Peter about being shown how to play music by following her heartbeat and then her visit to the Playhouse. She described every small detail from the copy of *The Tempest* left on the table, to her conversation about the scribbled names and numbers and the acrostic message possibly containing the name of Sir Francis Bacon. She omitted to tell him about the beautiful engraving of the double A A symbol and the picture of Athena, as she wanted to talk to her uncle in more depth about them.

Peter did not outwardly react to the account of her various discoveries, but knew he would have to talk to her more fully, at the appropriate occasion. He was aware of the involvement of Sir Francis Bacon in some of the plays and in a plan to publish all the works of the King's Men for posterity. He knew already about the acrostic message in *The Tempest* and the use of engravings. He suggested that they begin a game of chess and hopefully this would settle her mind after all the excitement of her day. He set out the chessboard and they both prepared to play.

'Why is the Goddess Athena called the Spear Shaker, Uncle?' Miranda asked as she made a move with her white pawn.

'That's a peculiar question, how did that come up in our conversation?' Peter asked in response, playing the black knight first, as he often did.

'Nathan thought that you might know, as the Goddess seems to be of importance to William Shakespeare.'

'One of the mysteries for all writers and musicians is what is the source of their inspiration? A wise person will know that it is not *who* wrote a particular piece, but what influenced them.'

Miranda digested his answer seeing how wise it was, as she moved another pawn. Peter then continued, considering the next chess piece to play.

'William Shakespeare learnt long ago this truth and through careful use of language and verse and story themes used since the beginning of time has aimed his life at a higher source of inspiration. This he identifies as Athena – the Goddess of wisdom, courage, inspiration, civilization, warfare, strength, strategy, female arts, crafts, justice and skill,' he added.

'Goodness, Uncle, I never realised!'

'These plays are not just random pieces of writing. It is true some of the scripts work better than others and some show pure genius, but William Shakespeare always sought to be true in everything he wrote to what he calls his muse. Her name is Pallas Athena and the Parthenon was built on the Acropolis of her namesake city, Athens, in her honour.'

Miranda and her uncle continued to play chess by the light of a large church candle and she let the wonder of the day play through her mind.

An Impromptu Rehearsal

*M*orning sunshine flooded into Miranda's room. She could not believe that she had slept so late and was a little disappointed. It was her last day at the apothecary before returning home to St. Albans for Christmas and she wanted to make the most of her remaining time.

There were voices in the study. She went to the landing and, looking down she was delighted to see Nathan standing next to Uncle Peter. Miranda could not hide a beaming smile as she came downstairs.

'Nathan has brought a message for you. You have an invitation to come to the Playhouse this evening to assist the musicians and scribes,' Peter said.

'And you can glean all you can about the new play.

You made quite an impression when you attended the writing in the library,' Nathan added.

'I am not sure. I need to return to St. Albans tomorrow!'

'Go tonight, it will be a great experience! You will not be here again until Twelfth Night and we can delay your departure in the morning if necessary,' Peter suggested.

'Thank you, Uncle.'

'I will leave you alone to discuss the details and ask Cathy to prepare breakfast for you both.'

Peter went to his work room, where ointments and powders needed to be prepared urgently for one of his friends.

'Can you tell me more about this evening?' Miranda asked Nathan excitedly.

'I have been told that several of the best theatre musicians in London have been invited to work on new music for the play *All Is True* about the life of King Henry VIII. I am not sure if William Shakespeare will be attending, but we will know when we get to the Playhouse. Can we have breakfast, as I am starving!'

'Of course, let's go and get some from the kitchen. Can you tell me any more about how the production is developing?'

'It seems that music is a very important part of the writing process and that is what is needed most at the moment. Beyond that I know very little.'

'Have you had time to think any more about the notes I found in the copy of *The Tempest*?'

'I have been working on them and discovered a few things.'

'Go on!'

'Guess what the meaning of the name FRANCIS is?'

'I have no idea!'

'The name means 'FREE' or 'Freeman' and is used in words such as Freemason. It may be a cryptic way to show the signature of Sir Francis Bacon.'

'But I thought Mr. Shakespeare wrote the play.'

'He did, but as far as I am beginning to understand he is the public face of the writing. There is also unseen collaboration from Sir Francis Bacon, which might account for the philosophical content of the play.'

'It is all making sense,' Miranda commented.

'How do you mean?' asked Nathan.

'Uncle Peter helped me understand why one A in the engraving I found in the copy of *The Tempest* is white and one A is shaded in the engravings printed in some of the folios of the plays. Possibly the first A is a symbol for William Shakespeare and the other shaded A is for Sir Francis Bacon?'

'I might be a bit slow, but ...'

'Well as you said one A is the public face of the plays and the other A is the unseen face.'

'Oh I see. Guess what the root numbers of the word FREE add up to?' Nathan asked.

'Don't say it is 33?' Miranda replied with another question.

'Yes. Using the alphabet that I showed you, the name Bacon and the word 'free' both make the same number – 33. So the word being included right at the end of the play could be like a signature?'

'Yes, I see but let's finish our breakfast. I have had enough of all these hidden ciphers!' Miranda sighed.

'Me too. I have a bit of time before I have to get back to the Playhouse, what would you like to do now?' Nathan asked.

'Could I help you rehearse for *Twelfth Night*?'

'How could you do that?'

'Well I have had a crazy idea. Why not let me act Viola and you act as the Duke?'

'But Viola is my part!'

'Yes, I know. But wouldn't you like to have the opportunity to see a girl playing the part, instead of a boy acting as a girl?'

'I am not sure. What do you have in mind?'

'Playwrights are constrained by the need to use boys for the female roles in the plays. Surely it would give you an entirely new perspective to work with a real girl in the role of Viola, rather than a playboy?'

'Yes, quite possibly, which part of the text do you want to rehearse?'

'When the Duke Orsino does not realise that his boy servant, Cesario, is actually Viola in disguise. You know the scene where Viola, dressed as the go-between Cesario, conveys to the Duke Orsino an impression of Olivia, the lady he is courting. Orsino does not realise that Viola is actually expressing her own love for the Duke through her description of Olivia's beauty.'

'I think that would be a great scene and would certainly give us a break from these ciphers and scribbled numbers. They have made my head giddy!'

'Some costume will add to the drama, don't you think?' Miranda asked, as she invited him up to the annex and dragged out a chest full of old clothes. Nathan discovered a cloak, a scarf and a fine stick to play the Duke. She found a waistcoat and breeches, and a floppy hat to complete her disguise as Cesario.

Once back downstairs and fully dressed in their costumes, Nathan began as the Duke Orsino:

My life upon't, young though thou art, thine eye
Hath stay'd upon some favour that it loves.
Hath it not, boy?

Miranda replies as Viola, disguised as Cesario:

A little, by your favour.

Duke Orsino: *What kind of woman is't?*

Viola: *Of your complexion.*

They continued to the end of the dialogue, enjoying the banter between Orsino and Viola. The Duke remains totally unaware that the boy servant is Viola in disguise.

Duke Orsino: *Then let thy love be younger*
than thyself,
Or thy affection cannot hold the bent:
For women are as roses, whose fair flower
Being once display'd, doth fall that very hour.

Viola: *And so they are: alas, that they are so:*
To die, even when they to perfection grow!

Miranda hesitated for a moment, not sure how the idea was working. 'How are we doing, Nathan? Your voice seems a little strange. Is everything alright?'

'My vocal chords seem to be a bit funny and my voice suddenly gets deeper without warning! I am sure it is not serious.'

'Can I ask Uncle Peter to prepare something for you?'

'Yes, but maybe later. I am so enjoying our acting together. I have never worked on a scene like this – with a real young lady! I have only worked with boys dressed as girls!'

'Can we continue, Nathan?' Miranda pleaded. 'There's that brilliant part where Viola, dressed as Cesario, tells the Duke that if he were a young woman, she would indeed love the Duke.'

'Of course!' Nathan said.

The Duke speaks about the depth of his own love for Olivia:

But mine is all as hungry as the sea,
And can digest as much. Make no compare
Between that love a woman can bear me
And that I owe Olivia.

In reply, Miranda skipped to the part where Viola says:
  … My father had a daughter lov'd a man,
  As it might be perhaps, were I a woman,
  I should your lordship.

Miranda looked into Nathan's eyes, but he did not realise that she was talking to him, through the play. She leant forward and kissed him gently on the cheek. Nathan stood rooted to the spot, the warmth of her kiss lingering on his face. He genuinely did not know what to say, but suddenly the reason why she had wanted them to act the scene dawned on him. They both stared at each other – the great globe of the Earth stood still.

'You have given me an idea,' Nathan exclaimed, grasping for something to say. 'At the end of the holiday we are playing an abridged version of the play at the grand house near High Holborn. It is called *Scenes from Twelfth Night* and William Shakespeare has given his permission for this to be presented at the Playhouse for all the staff who have worked over Christmas. Do you think your uncle would give his permission for the boy players I am working with to rehearse here at the apothecary? It will be the day you get back from St. Albans!'

'I think so. Will you let me play Viola for some of the rehearsal?'

'I don't mind at all, but I am not sure about the other boys.'

'Can you persuade them?'

'I am sure I can. But I must get back – there is much to do at the Playhouse.'

At the apothecary door Nathan completely surprised himself, and Miranda, by returning her earlier kiss.

Miranda was speechless.

'Your uncle will bring you to the Playhouse later. I will see you anon!'

Miranda was so stunned with Nathan's kiss that she just stood there rooted to the spot.

'Is everything alright?'

'Yes of course,' she finally said. 'I am looking forward to seeing you again tonight!'

She watched Nathan disappear into the night – back towards the lights of the monastery. The snow was now falling heavily as she returned to her attic room, her mind in a whirl. The plan to use the play to convey her feelings for Nathan had worked better than she had anticipated.

The Dance on the Stage

Later the same evening Miranda, and accompanied by her uncle, made her way to the Blackfriars Playhouse. There were few people out in the winter cold and the night was dark. When they saw the lights from the upper chamber of the old monastery it cheered them both up. She instinctively knew a magical evening lay ahead.

Once inside the theatre hall Miranda looked up and gasped at The Heavens suspended from the vaulted ceiling. She could not believe that she had so willingly climbed up there with Nathan. 'No wonder I felt giddy when I looked down!' she thought.

She waited with her uncle in the shadow of a stone arch at the rear of the theatre hall until they were called nearer to the stage. She was thrilled to see William Shakespeare and another gentleman dictating to a scribe. They were all seated upon large oak chairs on the centre platform and worked by the light of a large church candle.

'Who is that with Mr. Shakespeare, Uncle?'

'John Fletcher. The two are collaborating in completing the new play *All Is True.*'

Besides the chairs, the stage was set out with a few props and a selection of musical instruments. The theatre's large fireplaces, filled with burning wood, roared with life – their fiery glow bathing the lower walls of the auditorium in an orange light.

When the two stopped their dictation the atmospheric bubble that surrounded them vanished. A figure appeared out of the half-light of the tiring room and walked onto the stage.

Peter could hardly contain his surprise. 'That is Robert Johnson II, musical director for William Shakespeare and Court musician to King James. What is being planned must be very important!' he said, most impressed that on the stage were not only two of the finest playwrights in London, but also one of the most influential composers of the time. Johnson was a member of the King's own *Private Musick*.

Nathan was summoned to fetch Miranda. He bowed respectfully to her uncle and explained her role was to help the scribes with arranging the music sheets. She was free to move around the theatre and could listen-in on everything, whilst performing her duties.

Miranda's uncle left them both at the Playhouse. Outside, a freezing wind howled around the narrow lanes as he made his way home. He stood for a moment looking back at the old monastery – very content that Miranda was involved in the work of the evening.

Back inside, William Shakespeare and John Fletcher brought the musicians onto the stage and Miranda came closer. She overheard that they wanted to write another play and believed music, dance, and of course, poetry were a key to its success.

There was a quiet in the auditorium and Miranda was spellbound by the occasion. She looked around her at the great space and imagined angels and spirits flying across the vaulted ceiling. Behind the main stage there was an inner platform at the same level. Candles illuminated an image of the sun and the moon accompanied by the twelve astrological signs, beautifully painted upon panels.

At William Shakespeare's request, a musician was asked to accompany a solo boy singer who sang the playwright's favourite song *Full Fathom Five*, written by Robert Johnson for *The Tempest*. The song was still fresh in everyone's minds following the performance of the play in front of the King only a month before, and it evoked Prospero's resolve and majesty once again.

To Miranda's young eyes, William Shakespeare's facial expression changed, his posture straightened and a look of ancient wisdom played upon his face.

Unexpectedly, a messenger came on stage, disturbing the tranquility of the moment. Shakespeare left the stage, requesting Nathan to accompany him.

'Could it be another meeting with Sir Francis Bacon?' Miranda wondered, still intrigued by the mystery of his name being found in the play. She would have dearly loved to be a 'fly on the wall' in the room, but had to content herself with tidying up after the musicians and fetching refreshments when they were requested.

The Playhouse stage became a hive of activity as a new piece of music was being composed. John Fletcher dictated more lines to the scribes and a small group of musicians were being conducted by Robert Johnson.

After an hour their work was complete. John Fletcher sat to one side of the stage as the atmosphere settled and Robert Johnson prepared to conduct the musicians as a small orchestra in a newly composed *fantasia*. It was the musical setting for the words Miranda had been shown in the library from *All Is True*. She sat on a bench and listened entranced by the music. She looked up as she thought she saw something out of the corner of her eye – a pale glow in the high corner of the vaulted ceiling, just below The Heavens. After her experience of seeing the shimmering face of a king on the wall in the crypt she was becoming accustomed to such things at the Playhouse.

Visible only to her because of where she was sitting, Miranda saw a distinguished looking gentleman and William Shakespeare emerge from the steps leading up from the crypt. Miranda was convinced that this was Sir Francis Bacon. His similarity to Shakespeare in height and build were as she remembered from the two occasions she had seen them together. They stood side by side and listened to the music.

A boy player stood up and sang the lines from the play. Miranda reflected that William Shakespeare had not yet added another verse. The piece ended:

In sweet music is such art,
Killing care and grief of heart
Fall asleep, or hearing die.

The piece was performed beautifully and Miranda was so engrossed that she did not notice the two men leave the theatre hall. When she looked again in the direction of the tiring house, they were gone. The music was completed and the assembled musicians left the stage for refreshment.

Later, William Shakespeare returned. Clearly pleased with the piece, he sat with John Fletcher, discussing more parts for the play.

Nathan came back from the Abbot's study and catching Miranda's eye signalled that they should meet up in the small kitchen at the back of the stage.

'Was that Sir Francis Bacon with Mr. Shakespeare?' she asked, as they both huddled in the tiny room.

'Yes, there is no doubt about it! Now I have seen them for a second time I am sure they are working on some important project together. They met behind the closed door of the Abbot's study, only breaking to listen to the music for the new play. After they returned they continued their discussions a little longer and then Sir Francis left.'

'Did you glean anything?'

'As part of my duties I was asked to put away the books and papers when they finished their meeting and guess what?' Nathan began with a question.

'I don't know – was there another copy of *The Tempest*?'

'Yes, it was there before me on the table.'

'Did you look inside?'

'Couldn't help myself, could I?'

'And...'

'I looked for the scribbled notes and the acrostic message in the text. It was nowhere to be seen and even the lines spoken by Miranda that I learnt to perform before King James containing the letters B-A-Con were not there and the epilogue at the end was much shorter. FREE was not the final word. It was as if I was looking at a different play!'

'It must be another version. I will ask Uncle Peter – I am sure he will have an explanation.'

A boy player came to tell Miranda and Nathan that everyone was needed in the theatre hall. Their *tête-à-tête* ended for now.

After the success of the *fantasia* music for the new play, there was a celebratory atmosphere on stage.

'It is time for an adventure with improvised folk music!' Robert Johnson announced.

The gathering of musicians looked decidedly unimpressed. Improvisation was considered most improper, as it strayed from the exactness of religious musical form and was even considered by some as the work of the devil! William Shakespeare, true to his character, had little time for such short-sighted judgements and enjoyed these explorations into new music.

Robert Johnson invited one of the musicians, who he evidently knew well, to join him by the scribes table. The young man introduced himself as Christopher and, watched intently by the other musicians, carefully took a stringed instrument out of a battered case.

'This is a guitarra!' he announced, holding the instrument aloft. 'Made only a few months ago and brought here from Italy.'

The lines of the sound box were beautifully curved with mother-of-pearl inlay. Wood veneer patterns also decorated the fret board. Designed in Spain and copied in Venice, it was an instrument made with devotion and love.

'Please play a piece of your own choosing!' Robert Johnson urged.

'Very well. But I need to give the piece a brief introduction,' he said, resting his hand upon the guitarra.

He told how whilst he lived in Venezia (the Italian name for Venice) he had met and played with musicians from all over the Mediterranean and even from the Middle East. The City was a crucible for

The lines of the sound box were beautifully curved with mother-of-pearl inlay.
Wood veneer patterns also decorated the fret board.

experimentation and the development of styles of playing unheard of in London.

Starting slowly at first, Christopher's fingers connected delicately with the strings as if he were summoning the music. He then began to strum chords more boldly and gradually increased the tempo of his playing. This style was frowned upon by many as being crude in the extreme but there was something enchanting and evocative about his manner of playing that gradually quelled the judgement of his peers. Miranda was soon transported by the passion of the piece. She imagined the magical City she had been told about by her father, with its hidden squares and where musicians gathered on ornate bridges over emerald green canals. The playing became more and more intense and Christopher seemed to change. He appeared to became the vehicle for the passion of the piece as it built in intensity.

The music reached a fantastic crescendo and to the amazement of everyone William Shakespeare stood up from his chair and started to dance. The stiffness and tiredness in his legs disappeared, and he moved with ease. His reaction to the music was full of joy and intensity and displayed no inhibition or self-consciousness.

He looked to the side of the stage and indicated that Miranda join him in the dance. She hesitated momentarily and then joyfully jumped onto the stage. William Shakespeare took her hand and together they moved in a wide circle responding to the musician's spirited playing of the guitarra. Miranda discovered to her delight that she did not have to think about her dancing at all, as he guided her in every step. Some of the other musicians now joined in, providing accompaniment for the lone musician as he played, locked in a spell. John Fletcher, not known for his love of dancing, was also drawn into the frenzy. The music created flames of excitement – people moving in interconnecting circles, losing all sense of time. William Shakespeare then called Nathan to join him and smoothly and gently gave him Miranda's hands. He indicated that they should continue without him and he made his way over to the scribes, ensuring that the flow of the dance was not disturbed. The music continued until it reached its climax and then faded – the guitarra falling silent.

* * *

Later that evening, after Nathan had helped Miranda with her duties at the Playhouse and escorted her back to the apothecary, she decided that she must talk to her uncle about the discovery of the two different versions of *The Tempest*.

Despite the late hour, she found Uncle Peter reading in his study.

'I am glad you are home safely,' he said, as he invited her to sit by the fire. The flame of a large candle flickering on his desk cast a yellow light around the room.

'Uncle, can I ask you again about the copy of the play that I discovered in the library at the house near High Holborn?'

'Of course, have you found out something else?'

'Yes I have and it has been very confusing. Nathan, as part of his duties. was tidying away in the Abbot's study and found a copy of *The Tempest*. He knew all about what I had discovered previously and looked inside. He could not find Miranda's lines where the name B-A-Con had been hidden and the epilogue was much shorter and did not end with the word FREE. In fact it was quite a different version of the play from the one he had learnt for his performance at Court or I had seen.'

Peter paused before replying, as if considering carefully what he was about to say. He put down his book and gave his niece as much attention as he could.

'You already know that these days there is very little authors can do to restrict the publication of their work and many plays have been produced in different versions, many full of errors and with missing text. But this is not the reason in this case. I am sure you and Nathan have found two legitimate copies of *The Tempest,* both written by William Shakespeare, but one was intended for the public stage and one for quite a different purpose.'

'What could that be?' Miranda asked.

'Because I am a patron of the Playhouse I learn a great deal about the meetings that take place there. There is a plan for all the plays to be published in their entirety one day in preparation for the day when the Puritans close or pull down the theatres. This publication of the works would not be for profit, but financed by unnamed individuals and for several reasons. Firstly, it will ensure an authorised version of the plays exists for generations to come. Secondly, it is a way to communicate the philosophical ideas and secrets hidden in the plays. I believe that in the library at the grand house near

High Holborn you came across a special copy of the play designed for this project and for the performance in front of King James, at Court, but not for an open public audience,' he said pausing for a moment.

'King James?'

'Yes, both Queen Elizabeth was and King James is fully aware of Sir Francis Bacon's contribution to the plays. I know you would like me to tell you more now, but please try to be patient. You need to return to St. Albans tomorrow to spend Christmas with your father. Let us look forward to your return and the celebration of Twelfth Night,' he added.

Miranda thanked her uncle for providing another piece of the jigsaw. However she could not hide her disappointment as there was still more to understand. Reluctantly she went to bed.

After Miranda had gone to up to her attic room, Peter continued to ponder his neice's interest in the plays. He knew she was frustrated with not knowing fully the depth and extent of the working relationship between William Shakespeare and Sir Francis Bacon, but she needed to understand that it would always remain a secret while both men lived. It was planned that way and was necessary for the project to publish the plays for posterity. William Shakespeare would always be presented as the public face for the plays and Sir Francis Bacon's identity would remain hidden. Future generations may discover the truth, but in the turbulent and uncertain times in which they lived then it was not possible to reveal his role.

Peter stayed up for another hour and wrote his niece a letter to explain her tasks for the holiday. He bookmarked certain pages for her to read and research from a play written over ten years ago by William Shakespeare. Called *The History of King Henry IV* it was still one of the most popular productions in the repertoire of the King's Men and contained some of the most memorable characters the playwright ever created such as Hotspur, Falstaff and Hal. The play includes a radical stage innovation where scenes set in a public house allow for the inclusion of comic episodes within the deadly serious political history. However one of these tavern scenes was created for a very special edition of the play rarely performed, which Peter wanted his niece to discover as it contained probably the clearest identification of Sir Francis Bacon in any of the plays.

Francis

After the journey from London to the family home in the City of St. Albans, Miranda was soon preparing for the Christmas celebrations. The house felt terribly lonely without her mother and she missed her friends at the Blackfriars, so she busied herself setting up rooms and helping the maid prepare food and treats for the festive season. Her father's work as a goldsmith kept him very busy right up to the start of Christmastide and so Miranda also had time to immerse herself in reading the play her uncle had given her to research.

She was unfamiliar with the breadth of William Shakespeare's history dramas and was amazed at the complexity of *The History of King Henry IV*.

As hoped by her uncle, she discovered a character known as Francis – a bartender employed in a public house frequented by the main characters. It was clear to Miranda that, in the scene where he plays a main part, his name Francis appears far too often to be natural. Using the tools Nathan had shown her she searched for ciphers in the text. There were no obvious anagrams or acrostics, so she hunted for numbers instead. Using the Elizabethan alphabet code she tried in vain to find anything of note. A little frustrated she re-read the scene several times and then hit upon a possible clue. She decided to count the number of times the name appeared on the single page in which the scene was printed. She could not believe her luck and was thrilled to find that it totalled thirty-three – the personal cipher number of Sir Francis Bacon.

She felt a little bit like a spy who had cracked a secret code. She checked her addition several times before satisfying herself that the name was there in print exactly thirty-three times. The more she read the text the more it was obvious that the playwright had used very awkward scriptwriting to achieve this end – such as: *Anon, Francis? No, Francis, but tomorrow,*

Francis; or, Francis, a-Thursday; or indeed, Francis, when thou wilt. But Francis! It was clearly artificial, even if it made for an extremely comical and entertaining scene.

Believing she had found an important clue Miranda searched through the same scene over and over again. It struck her that the setting for the public house sequence at The Boar's Head Tavern might be a signpost to Sir Francis – the *boar* being one of his family's symbols. Searching through the play she found an ornate engraving that clearly included this animal – confirming her belief. She also judged that the scene was trying to say something more. 'Could it be a reflection of Sir Francis Bacon's state of mind?' she wondered.

The more she read the dialogue in the tavern scene, she felt it might actually be revealing the contradictions that Sir Francis Bacon felt in not being able to pursue what he really loved in life – a public role in the theatre. He may have been deeply frustrated that his involvement had to be concealed because of his position in society – actors, public theatres and playwrights being seen to belong to a social class below his own.

Miranda could not wait to get back to Blackfriars to thank her uncle and tell Nathan all about a further play that so clearly identified Sir Francis Bacon.

* * *

Christmas arrived and as was the tradition it was dominated by church and taking Holy Communion. Their nearest place of worship and where her father, Thomas, served as a warden was the Cathedral near the top of the hill in St. Albans. The late hours of Christmas Eve were the most magical – the flaming beacons at the entrance welcomed the town folk arriving through the snow in the darkness. It was a beautiful sight to behold.

Once the succession of church services was over Miranda and her father enjoyed time at home and walking in the surrounding countryside. Thomas spoilt her terribly and every day there was a special outing or the maid cooked a sumptuous meal. It was on one of these excursions that Miranda's current interest in Sir Francis Bacon received an added boost from an unexpected source. Thomas took her for a stroll near Gorhambury in St. Albans and Miranda was overjoyed to find that it was the summer home for the Bacon family. In fact Sir Francis and the City of St. Albans were linked in all sorts of ways that Miranda was unaware of and Thomas knew a great deal about the knight and was very proud that the famous astrologer, philosopher and statesman had lived in their home City.

When they were comfortably settled back at home, Thomas told her that whilst a student at Cambridge, Bacon became thoroughly disillusioned with the whole system of thought and teaching there. He left, believing there was nothing more the University could teach him and subsequently became respected as a visionary and a great thinker, philosopher and writer. It was even known, if not generally, that he contributed significantly to William Shakespeare's works and particularly the history plays, including the one Miranda was currently reading. She was particularly fascinated that he was involved in the decision to characterise King Richard III as a deformed and evil character. This was not how the ruler was shown in many history books and this pointed to the use of the mummers of the King's Men and their special skills to explore this side of his personality. Miranda recalled vividly her experience of witnessing the trainees in combat in the crypt at Blackfriars and the malevolent character played so realistically by one of the boys.

'Do you know what Sir Francis finds so valuable about the theatre?' Miranda asked her father.

'I believe that one of his ideals is to discover truth and practice philanthropy and, like the Ancient Greeks, to teach wisdom through entertainment. This is what possibly draws him to form a partnership with William Shakespeare. It is necessary that the playwright be the public face and Bacon the unseen contributor. William Shakespeare is the prolific writer and skilled dramatist and Bacon the master of philosophy – both needing each other to reach beyond their limits.'

During their conversations Miranda was able to tell her father about Nathan and the Blackfriars Playhouse and the extraordinary opportunities she had been given to attend the playwriting by William Shakespeare. She was delighted that he had fewer objections to her association with the boy players than she feared. He recognised that apprentices to the highly valued King's Men must be very talented and he was thrilled that she had any association with the work of a great playwright such as Shakespeare. However he counselled that she must accept that the identity of Sir Francis Bacon would always remain hidden where any association with the work of William Shakespeare was concerned. It was a fact of life given the society in which they lived and would never change. An active role in performing or writing for the theatre was considered too common for members of the King's Inner Courts or the aristocracy. It was simply out of the question. Miranda realised that her father was echoing her uncle's counsel that she concentrate on her love of the plays and not the fruitless exercise of identifying Sir Francis Bacon's role in their writing. He was a knight of the realm and an eminent scholar and she must accept that, unlike William Shakespeare, she would never meet him. He would always remain veiled and out of reach.

As a parting gift Thomas gave her one of Sir Francis Bacon's books called *In felicem memoriam Elizabethanae*. Written in 1609, it was a eulogy for Queen Elizabeth I. He thought it would give his daughter a wider perspective on the great man's work and the book was a good example of the writings the philosopher could or would publish in his own name.

✻ ✻ ✻

Miranda returned to Blackfriars feeling much more settled. She was determined to concentrate on her Latin, playing the lute and learning more about the plays. She was beginning to be in total awe of the immensity of what William Shakespeare had achieved, even if this was with the assistance of eminent people or scholars – known or unknown. She arrived in time for a light dinner with Jane and they enjoyed catching up, but were both so tired from their journeys. Their uncle also arranged for Cathy to make up a bed so that they could again share the attic room and very soon they were both asleep.

The morning of Twelfth Night was bright and fresh and the weather was returning to being bitterly cold, after the brief warm spell. Nathan and John and three other boy performers were arriving for an early afternoon rehearsal at the apothecary of their mini-production *Scenes from Twelfth Night*. True to Nathan's word, Miranda was taking his role and participating as Viola in the rehearsal. Nathan wanted to see the reaction of the boys to her interpretation of the part – playing it as a real girl, and not as a boy dressed as one! Also, as it was Christmas, it was an opportunity for a party before a performance at six o'clock at the grand house near to High Holborn.

Jane came downstairs a little after her cousin and found Miranda in the garden room reading. Over breakfast Miranda told Jane about the afternoon's play and the preparations that needed to be made for the little get-together. She also let her know about the part of Viola that she was acting.

'But I thought you were not permitted to act on the stage!' Jane exclaimed.

'This is only a private performance at home. There won't be any audience except the other boy players!'

'Which boys did you say?' Jane asked showing more interest.

'I didn't, but there will be Nathan and John, whom you have already met, and three other apprentices from the King's Men – Richard, Henry and Alexander.'

'What wondrous, wondrous news! I think this will be my best Twelfth Night ever!' Jane said, thinking more of the boys than the play.

* * *

A little after midday Nathan, John and the three new

boys arrived at the apothecary. As was the custom of the day, the new lads introduced themselves with great propriety to Miranda and Jane. The girls sat by the fire like two princesses at Court, Jane staring at them with delight. The young actors were all trained to play female roles, and they were more handsome than most young men of their age. Also their flamboyant personalities, developed by years in the theatre and mixing with acting troupes, greatly appealed to her.

Richard came forward and bowed gracefully. He told the girls proudly that he was already well known as a master jester, even at the young age of twelve. Richard had been taught by his father, who was a mute. During his upbringing they only communicated using gestures and this had given the young lad a unique experience of mime and facial expressions. He cleverly added to his self-introduction by giving Miranda and Jane, each in turn, a mime of their individual nature. For Jane he impersonated her fluttering eyes and Miranda her playing of the lute. The girls thought this was very amusing.

Henry, a slightly older boy of thirteen was next to make his introduction. Boy players could communicate, if required, with astonishing grace. Born the son of an East London tanner, Henry's accent betrayed his humble origins. Fully aware this would do him no favours in higher circles, he had spent every spare hour of his youth cultivating an eloquent and delicate speaking voice. This had earned him the most desired acting roles for boy players in the London theatre scene. Miranda and Jane beamed with delight at his courteous manners.

The last boy to introduce himself was Alexander. He was famous for his role as Juliet in the well-known tragedy by William Shakespeare. He was by far the prettiest of the boys and would be playing Olivia in the production of Twelfth Night when it was performed at the grand house and at the Blackfriars.

Nathan suggested they use the costumes from the chest, already brought down from the annexe, and after rummaging around they found some sort of accessory or outfit for everyone. Miranda was now suitably attired as the messenger from the Duke Orsino. Nathan hoped the role reversal when Viola is disguised as the young man Cesario, would interest the boys – being that they would never have seen an actual girl play the part.

Viola (disguised as Cesario) is in conversation with Olivia.

Viola: *Good madam, let me see your face.*

Olivia: *Have you any commission from your lord to negotiate with my face? You are now out of your text: but we will draw the curtain and show you the picture. (Unveiling) Look you, sir, such a one I was this present. Is't not well done?*

Viola: *Excellently done, if God did all.*

Olivia: *'Tis in grain, sir; 'twill endure wind and weather.*

Viola: *'Tis beauty truly blent, whose red and white Nature's own sweet and cunning hand laid on.*
Lady, you are the cruell'st she alive
If you will lead these graces to the grave
And leave the world no copy.

When the scene finished there was a silence in the room. Miranda played the role much better than the boys had expected. Alexander was greatly impressed – he had never worked opposite a girl in the play and found the experience gentler and more natural than he had anticipated. He reflected that William Shakespeare was an even greater writer than he had appreciated to have been able to create such a depth of sensitivity. It was as if he knew that one day a female actor would play the role on stage. Nathan, John, Richard and Henry all applauded.

Richard, the most astute of the boy players, could not fail to see that if it had not been the accepted convention of the day that boys play the female roles, they would all be out of a job! Viola's qualities as a woman were better played by Miranda, even though her acting was no match for the boy players' training. He began to question whether the prettiest or most talented boy player could ever match a young woman properly prepared to act on the stage.

Peter popped his head in, attracted by the sound of applause. He was very surprised to see Miranda dressed as a boy, but Nathan soon reassured him that it was for a suitable purpose and Peter was delighted that her performance was so much appreciated and that she was concentrating on her love of the plays again.

During the small party that followed Miranda took Nathan aside to tell him about her discoveries while she was away in St. Albans. He was absolutely riveted by her account of everything she had uncovered and was totally unaware of the scene included in the play that showed the name Francis thirty-three times. He listened carefully as she passed on the counsel that her father had given her about Sir Francis Bacon's identity. Nathan agreed that they would be wise to respect the seriousness of the anonymity of the philosopher, even though it had been exciting to speculate on his contributions to the plays.

It was already dark when the boys left. It was going to be a busy evening for them all. After the performance at High Holborn they would be coming back to present the same show at the Blackfriars to end Twelfth Night. A special evening had been arranged by the patrons and friends of the Playhouse for all the boys who had worked over Christmas.

Miranda kissed Nathan before he left and John was delighted with a hug from Jane. Alexander, Richard and Henry bowed courteously to both girls and the five boys headed off into the sleet that was now falling heavily.

The Falling Tower

It was past nine on the same evening as Peter carefully guided his nieces Miranda and Jane along the cobbled lane in the snow. It was very dark beyond the apothecary's lights and he was glad when they reached the monastery, where flaming torches burned at the entrance. Through the high windows they could see the welcoming glow of the candlelit chandeliers in the theatre hall and they were looking forward to spending the final hours of Twelfth Night at the Playhouse. They joined the staff, patrons and guests making their way up the stone steps to the grand meeting chamber and Peter recognised a fellow supporter of the theatre and was soon chatting with him. Miranda and Jane walked beside them a little impatiently. They were keen to catch up with their boy player friends after their performance at High Holborn.

Inside the main hall large roaring fires comforted the guests. Logs spat, crackled and cackled like demons – the magic of the final day of Christmas in the air. Miranda and Jane warmed themselves by one of the hearths, hoping to see the boys, and then unexpectedly the doors to the side of the hall dramatically burst open. To the sound of trumpets, a group of gaudily dressed men entered laughing and shouting as they duelled with swords.

The old monastery was the home of a fencing school that often provided its services for large battle scenes in the plays. As a Christmastide gift, trainees had offered to entertain everyone to start the party. They recreated the opening scene from William Shakespeare's play *Romeo and Juliet,* where the opposing families of Capulets and Montagues challenge each other to a fight. Everyone was aware that the duels were not real, but at close quarters the combat was noisy and frightening. They had spare blades and invited the boy players to join in. Miranda spotted Nathan and John on stage and they were acquitting themselves very well mock-fighting with the swordsmen, whilst everyone else cheered them on.

More trumpets sounded. The duelling ceased and everyone was invited to help themselves to the food and drink set out on tables in the adjoining hallway. The custom on the eve of the twelfth day of Christmas, known as Twelfth Night or Epiphany, was to reverse roles and true to this tradition the patrons of the theatre became the servants of the staff who had worked so hard all year and over the season. Christopher, the musician who had played for the dance on the stage at the writing for *All Is True*, arrived with his musician friends and as a treat for everyone performed songs to accompany the feast.

Miranda found Nathan sitting at the side of the stage. He was rather exhausted after the fencing. She asked him how the performance at High Holborn had faired.

'It was excellent and the guests really enjoyed the play, but I seem to be completely losing my voice!' he confided in her. It was not the sort of admission he wanted to make in front of any of the boys, but was relaxed speaking about it with Miranda.

'I'll go and find some warm mead and honey,' she said, suggesting that Nathan go and get changed into his costume. He nodded in agreement and then made his way backstage. It was obvious his voice was of great concern to him.

More boy players started to arrive – some looking very tired. Christmas was a busy time for all actors and most had only just finished their last performance of the season. They were greeted with food and warm drinks by the patrons and friends and the prospect of a party and a chance to enjoy some entertainment soon brought the fire back into their eyes.

Beyond the main theatre, the light was very dull and as she approached the tiring house Miranda bumped into one of the visiting boy actors.

'Nathan, I see you are in costume already. You make a wonderful Viola!' the boy said cheekily. It was unknown for a young woman to be allowed this close to the tiring house and so his assumption over Miranda's identity was quite natural. Also the rule backstage was for her to wear a hood, which partially obscured her face.

'I...' Miranda was speechless, realising that the boy thought that she was Nathan already in costume.

'Lost for words?' the boy asked.

Just at this point, Nathan appeared through the doorway, dressed as Viola.

'My goodness, there are *two* Violas!' the boy exclaimed.

Miranda and Nathan stood side by side, as the bemused boy studied them. They were the same height and did look so much alike that anyone could have mistaken them for twins. Amused by the situation, Miranda did not speak, intent on not revealing that she was really a girl. The boy returned to the theatre hall still a little bewildered.

'Are you ready yet for the performance, Nathan?' she asked.

'I am fine apart from my voice. I am hoping this drink will settle my vocal chords! I need to prepare so please go and sit with your uncle in the audience.'

Miranda agreed reluctantly and gave Nathan the warm mead before watching him return into the tiring house. Trumpets sounded for everyone to take their seats. Boys, patrons and friends all eagerly found places on the benches and the theatre hall was soon buzzing with anticipation. Mysteriously however, there was no activity on stage and no sign of anyone in the wings.

'That's strange – why haven't they announced the play?' Miranda thought, as she squeezed next to Uncle Peter at the end of a row.

'I am fetching some more mead for Nathan and will be back shortly!' Miranda said to her uncle, instinctively knowing that something was wrong and making an excuse to go and find him.

'But…' Peter called out.

Miranda was already on her way to the tiring house.

Backstage the boys were gathered around a distraught Nathan, who sat with his head in his hands. It was obvious that his voice was now not just hoarse, but it was undergoing a complete transformation. He could hide the problem with his vocal chords no longer. Henry had already weighed up the situation and knew that Nathan's voice had finally broken and his days as a boy player were over. However with a lively and anticipant audience front of stage the show had to go on.

'We will need a new theme for the production!' Henry said to his colleagues.

To give everyone time to think, Richard and John volunteered to go on stage and warm up the audience as two Fools, singing songs and telling jokes. The popularity of such double acts had increased immensely since King James employed his own pair of jesters known mysteriously as 'The Three Loggerheads'. While the two boys did a splendid job on stage, an urgent discussion continued backstage.

Just at that moment Miranda arrived at the door to the tiring house, carrying more warm mead for Nathan from the kitchen. Her appearance gave Henry an idea.

'Miranda, you must play Viola for the show and replace Nathan!' Henry was convinced from this afternoon's party at the apothecary that she knew the part well and would not discredit the boys. Tonight was a private event and as such the convention that a female could not publicly act on stage would not be broken.

'We could use the *role reversal* theme of Epiphany and present scenes from William Shakespeare's plays that celebrate how young women have used the disguise of dressing as a man to achieve their goal. This will mean we can shorten the number of scenes from *Twelfth Night*. Our small troupe has a huge repertoire to draw upon so it won't be a problem,' Alexander suggested.

'Yes. Richard can recite a speech as Julia from the play *The Two Gentlemen of Verona* and John can play

Rosalind from *As You Like It*. I can play Imogen from the play *Cymbeline* and we can reduce the lines that Miranda will need to play as Viola in place of Nathan. We must omit the part with the Duke Orsino, but we can keep some of her lines with Olivia. For the first time on our stage a girl, rather than a boy, will act the role. It is most exciting!' Henry added dramatically.

'Do you think it will work?' Nathan asked the other boys.

'Of course, it is a splendid plan, but how do you feel about it, Nathan?' Alexander asked.

'It is always hard to accept change, but as one door closes another opens! My days as a boy player may be over, but I can now take my place in the adult theatre troupe. I shall help everyone tonight backstage and encourage Miranda from the wings. I am sure she will be fantastic!' Nathan said graciously.

'Well done, Nathan. Alexander will be playing Olivia opposite her as already rehearsed today and he will make sure she is supported!' Henry added.

'Is it settled then?' Alexander asked.

'It depends if Miranda is willing to participate,' said Nathan, turning to her.

'It is a wonderful opportunity, even if it has come about through the timing of Nathan's voice changing!' Miranda responded.

'Don't worry about being recognised. Nathan and you are so alike and if required we shall simply say you are a visiting boy player. The people in the audience are our friends and will not question us. Wear this larger than usual moustache, that will help as well to disguise your face,' Henry reasoned.

'It would be a dream come true, I'll get ready immediately!' Miranda said as she took Nathan's costume and applied the moustache.

She was given a separate room to change in whilst the other boys got ready for their own female roles. She was disappointed that her dream of acting on the stage with Nathan, as the Duke Orsino, was as yet unfulfilled, but was delighted to have this opportunity nonetheless.

Inside the theatre hall, Uncle Peter sat with Jane beside him, enjoying Richard and John's warm-up for the play. Unexpectedly he felt someone tap him on the shoulder. He turned and could not believe his eyes. There standing at the end of the row, with a female partner at his side, was Miranda's father, Thomas.

The personal matter that he had attended to over Christmas had clearly been resolved much earlier than expected. Peter guessed that it concerned the lady who was now taking her place next to them on the bench.

'Where is Miranda?' Thomas asked Peter.

'Nathan, the boy player whom she befriended, is not well. His throat is troubling him and she is assisting with warm drinks.'

'Surely she is not allowed backstage?'

'Fear not, Thomas, it is totally appropriate, even though it is most unusual. She has been given extraordinary access to the Playhouse over the last year and does attend to the players from time to time.'

'Yes, she began to tell me at home in St. Albans over Christmas. But I did not realise how many friends she had made. I am happy as long as she is safe.'

The main show with the theme of Epiphany was announced. No one in the audience had been expecting a specific play and the prospect of such a wide selection of entertaining scenes was greeted with great excitement. Some junior actors worked beneath the stage, creating special effects – a rolling cannon ball for thunder, and metal sheets used to create the sound of lightning. Two others waited in The Heavens – the effects box high above the stage where Nathan and Miranda had explored over the summer.

Unbeknownst to anyone, William Shakespeare stood in the shadows at the side of the stage. He had been attracted to the theatre hall by the audience's cheering and laughter. Working alone in the study and waiting for a visitor, he welcomed a break from his current concerns. The show suited his mood well and he stood absorbed as he observed each individual performance from the plays he had written. Richard's Julia reminded him of the excitement he had felt at completing the play *The Two Gentlemen of Verona* over twenty years before. It was his first public success and brought him to the attention of important people and then to Sir Francis Bacon, the man he was about to meet with.

William Shakespeare continued to watch all the boys. He enjoyed John's Rosalind and Henry's playing of Imogen from the play *Cymbeline* was as entertaining as ever. The next character was one of his favourite female heroines. However he did not immediately recognise the young actor who came onto the stage to act Viola, dressed as the go-between Cesario, from the play *Twelfth Night*, showing remarkable femininity and sensitivity for a boy. He knew it was not Nathan.

Miranda entered, recalling the many times she had rehearsed the part alone or with Nathan. Alexander, who was playing Olivia, knew she was nervous and gave her a friendly wink to reassure her.

'My goodness that boy looks remarkably like Miranda,' Thomas commented to Peter and Jane.

'It can't be!' Uncle Peter said emphatically, concealing his real thoughts. He knew it was his niece on stage.

Thomas accepted his brother's assertion that it could not be Miranda. Under the dim light of the candles in the chandeliers above the stage, they assumed the actor wearing a large hat and false moustache was Nathan – believing that he must have recovered sufficiently to play a small part in the production. If not it must be a visiting actor.

William Shakespeare however recognised the player as the young girl who had popped out of a chest on stage so unexpectedly during the rehearsals for *The Tempest* at the beginning of the year. She was the niece of one of his most loyal patrons and had assisted excellently as an attendant at the playwriting for *All Is True*. He had no idea why she was replacing Nathan, but presumed there was a very good reason for her now appearing as Viola on the stage of the Blackfriars. Fascinated and intrigued, he listened carefully to her acting. Miranda acquitted herself extremely well and the scene was performed with commitment and sensitivity. He was impressed how competently she worked with Alexander, playing Olivia. The scene had clearly been rehearsed and she knew her lines inside out, which pleased him.

Continuing the soliloquies, the Playhouse fell silent as Miranda recited Viola's famous speech from Act II, Scene 2 of *Twelfth Night*, still dressed as the boy Cesario. It was fortunate that she was unaware that William Shakespeare stood in the shadows by the stage, or she might have run off in fright. Pleased at the passion and intensity with which she acted the scene, he reflected upon the lines part way through Viola's speech:

I am the man: if it be so, as 'tis,
Poor lady, she were better love a dream.
Disguise, I see thou art a wickedness,
Wherein the pregnant enemy does much.
How easy is it for the proper false
In women's waxen hearts to set their forms!

Miranda paused, as if knowing someone was listening. She continued to the final lines:

And she, mistaken, seems to dote on me:
What will become of this? As I am man,
My state is desperate for my master's love:
As I am woman (now alas the day!)
What thriftless sighs shall poor Olivia breathe?
O time, thou must untangle this, not I.
It is too hard a knot for me t'untie.

The play he wrote almost ten years before prompted Shakespeare to contemplate one of the prophecies he had made: that women would one day be free to act upon the stage. As Viola's words in the soliloquy stated – it was a *knot* that needed to be untangled, but he knew that the relentless power of time would make things eventually come to be. He was sure not only of the place that women would one day take as actors in public theatre but also believed profoundly in the destiny of English as the most influential language on earth.

William Shakespeare returned to the study and as part of his daily contemplation, he took a tarot card out from the box on the shelf. He mused upon the picture it contained of a tower being struck by lightning with two people falling to the ground, escaping the flames. Called *The Falling Tower,* the card matched his feelings today. The play he associated with the image was his yet unfinished *The Life of Timon of Athens.* It had been a

The play he associated with the image was his yet unfinished
The Life of Timon of Athens

difficult piece to write, as it has a bitter and negative theme, but he hoped that it would eventually rival his great tragedy, *King Lear*. He recalled a speech by Timon that summed up well the life of a playwright. Like many of his competitors William Shakespeare was criticised for using the wealth of existing stories and plays by other authors. However in his own view many of these writings were pedestrian in their execution and he knew that through his genius as a playwright he could endow them with distinction and sometimes with a greatness that surpassed their original form. His theatre troupe successfully brought them to the stage and transformed the insipid melodramas of many other writers into the engaging and successful plays they were renowned for. 'This is why we are the King's Men,' he reflected proudly. Timon speaks:

... I'll example you with thievery.
The sun's a thief, and with his great attraction
Robs the vast sea. The moon's an arrant thief,
And her pale fire she snatches from the sun.
The sea's a thief, whose liquid surge resolves
The moon into salt tears. The earth's a thief,
That feeds and breeds by a composture stolen.

William Shakespeare paused for a moment before continuing a little further through the speech:

Each thing's a thief.
The laws, your curb and whip, in their rough power
Have unchecked theft...

Sir Francis Bacon, the playwright's visitor, arrived – as always through the underground tunnel that connected the Playhouse with the Blackfriars Gate-House. It was now well past midnight and within their different spheres it had been a busy Christmas for both men.

William shared with him the experience of listening to scenes from some of their best known plays during the boys' production. He admitted to Francis that he did not feel that the new play *All Is True* was shaping up to match the greatness of their previous works. He even felt that it would somehow bring disaster to the troupe. Something had profoundly changed and he sensed a period of his life was coming to a close.

Sir Francis did not interrupt him. He also knew that the twenty-one years he had tutored William Shakespeare had been a unique opportunity for them to push back the boundaries of playwriting together.

These years had been some of the richest times of his life, but he too knew there was change in the air.

Sir Francis looked at the tarot card of *The Falling Tower* that lay on the desk from the pack he had once given his pupil, and reflected on its prophesy. They both knew that this golden age of theatre would not last forever and the Puritans would one day have their way and pull down the playhouses of London. The two continued their discussions knowing that they would be meeting for many hours yet. Their current concern was the preservation of the plays for future generations.

Backstage everything had been tidied away for the boys. Miranda kissed Nathan, thanked him for his encouragement and looked forward to his first performance as a member of the King's Men troupe. Assured that they would meet again soon, Miranda went to find Uncle Peter and Jane. Her hood now lowered and her face fully visible, no one identified her as an actor and the costume she had worn for the performance was well hidden beneath her cloak.

To her surprise and delight she saw her father and then was fearful that he must have recognised her on stage. She had no idea how or why he was at the

Playhouse, but they hugged warmly – no mention of her participation in the play was made. It was assumed Nathan had been the player on stage.

'There is someone I want you to meet,' Thomas said as he introduced the lady standing close-by.

'I am glad your friend recovered well,' the attractive lady said warmly, as she turned to face Miranda.

Miranda detected a slight smile on her face – as if the lady knew it had been her on stage rather than Nathan, but had decided to keep Miranda's little secret safe.

'Yes, quite recovered, ma'am,' she replied.

Thomas took Miranda to one side and told her what had happened since she had returned to the apothecary over Christmas. She did not know what to think at the prospect of a stepmother in her life, but Miranda always listened to her instincts and found she was settled and happy. Mary did look ever so lovely and it had been many months since Miranda had seen her father so well.

'I hope you managed to see some of the performance from the wings?' Uncle Peter asked, with a grin.

'Yes, Uncle, I particularly enjoyed the soliloquies, and Nathan's small contribution – made short due to his voice.'

'Might I suggest you wipe that little bit of moustache from your face and wrap up warmly, it is very cold outside!' he said pointing at the untied chord around her neck.

Miranda felt the small remnant of the moustache still stuck to her skin and looking down was horrified to see the golden buttons of the costume she wore to play Cesario protruding through the opening in her cloak.

'Yes, Uncle I will indeed!' she said, realising that he knew full well what she had been up to on stage.

Miranda would never be aware that William Shakespeare had seen her performance that evening and her acting of Viola would remain one of the Blackfriars' many secrets.

* * *

Postscript

Many Years Later

It was a warm September afternoon in 1667, as Thomas helped his mother descend the steps outside the small theatre in the Haymarket, the home of the Duke's Company. At the age of 71, Miranda was not only exceptionally old for the times in which she lived, but she was also extraordinarily healthy. The only explanation she could offer for her continuing stamina and wellbeing was a fulfilled life and a good diet and never forgetting the ways of thinking that she had learnt from William Shakespeare with the help of Nathan.

Since those days of adventure at the Playhouse much had changed in England and particularly in London. As foreseen in the story, the Globe Theatre was burnt down during a performance of *All Is True* (The Life of King Henry VIII) in 1613. Although it was re-built, William Shakespeare's work in London as a playwright came finally to an end. The grand meeting chamber that had housed the Playhouse was demolished in 1655 and the remains of the ancient monastery at Blackfriars finally fell to the flames of the great fire that destroyed a large part of the Old City and the lofty wooden tower of St. Paul's Cathedral in 1666. All that was left of the Playhouse was a small stone wall and part of the graveyard.

For almost forty years the old monastery had witnessed, within its walls, the greatest flowering of theatre to ever take place in England – continuing uninterrupted, until the Puritans were finally granted the right to enforce the closure of the London theatres during the Civil War in 1642. When Charles II granted licenses for new theatre companies as part of the Restoration of the Monarchy, which started in 1660, the King's Men sadly were no more. However, the plays of William Shakespeare lived on – made possible in part by their publication of the *First Folio* in 1623, from the playwright's original writings, as overseen by Sir Francis Bacon.

There was a noise of laughter and the door of the theatre opened behind Miranda. Out stepped her granddaughter Anne, who had just changed out of her costume for the small part she was playing in the play *King Lear*. She held the hand of a handsome young man, who looked delighted with her in every respect. Not only was she intelligent and lovely, but she showed great promise as an actress. Miranda could not hold back a small tear as she thought of Nathan, her late husband, and how the dream they had often talked about had finally come true – women could now freely act on the public stage.

* * *

References for
Miranda's meetings with Shakespeare

The importance of the play *The Tempest* and the
First Folio (1623)

The Tempest is the last play accredited solely to William Shakespeare and was first performed at Court for King James I in November 1611. It is curious that although written near the very end of his career, *The Tempest* opens the complete works published as the *First Folio* in 1623, seven years after the playwright's death. The story of Prospero and Miranda as castaways on an Enchanted Island clearly contains ideas fundamental to the threads of philosophy that weave throughout all of Shakespeare's plays.

The *First Folio* was almost certainly financed by a private group of individuals linked with members of the King's Men and published for posterity, rather than for commercial gain. This group, possibly secretly led and advised by Sir Francis Bacon, saw the publication of the works as a philanthropic act for the benefit of future generations, rather than a contemporary audience.

The Tempest therefore provided a fitting way to open the set of writings.

The tale of the shipwrecked members of the royal family finding reconciliation with the once exiled magician and his daughter is profound in its meaning and simplicity. The notion of the 'castaway' as a way of shedding light on our own journey to salvation is also powerful and provocative and sets the scene for a collection of plays that invite analysis at many levels.

The thirty-six plays of the *First Folio* have since provided the world with core themes and story lines for thousands of films, books and writings and remains today the greatest collection of plays and poetry every written and an unending source of interest around the world.

The English Theatre Renaissance

Miranda's meetings with Shakespeare is set in the richest and most creative period of theatrical production in English history. Between 1575 and the mid 1620s playwrights working alone or in short-lived partnerships created many thousands of plays in and around London. Only a small percentage of the plays still survive in printed form. The incredible flowering of theatre works during these fifty years was stimulated by the interest and patronage of Queen Elizabeth I and her successor King James I.

New playwrights and authors found an outlet for their work in London's many open air and public house theatres, where eager audiences gathered. The sudden explosion of creativity and rapid expansion of new knowledge at this time can be compared to the growth of the Internet in our modern times.

The Blackfriars was unique as a Playhouse at the time and we can only imagine the atmosphere that was present in the grand hall of the ancient monastery only lit by candles; undisturbed by traffic noise or the bustle of our modern technological and industrial society. In a world without cinema or TV the theatre was also a very important arena for the communication of ideas and news. People were able to learn new views of history, and about the world beyond England and Europe becoming more and more accessible through the explorations of the great mariners of this age.

It is the author's view that the naming by the King's Men of their most well-known theatre *The Globe* was a radical idea in the late 1500s. Some authorities at the time would still not even acknowledge that 'the world was round'. Shakespeare would have heard of Sir Francis Drake's explorations around the world, proving the earth was not flat. Islands such as Tenerife and the Bahamas were newly discovered and his plays were often set in similarly foreign and exotic places; this may have been an attraction for people to see plays at the Globe. Galileo, the famous Italian astronomer, also discovered by 1610 that the earth was not the centre of the universe, but revolved around the sun. As Shakespeare was writing his last plays at the Blackfriars, peoples' views of the world, religion and ways of life were being transformed.

Blackfriars Playhouse

A converted Dominican monastery near Water Lane in London was the site for the Blackfriars Playhouse used by the King's Men and William Shakespeare from 1608. Unlike the Globe, the whole audience could be seated and it was uniquely located close to the Old City, in an area known as a 'Liberty'. Ancient rights gave the King's Men freedom to operate under the watchful eyes of the puritanical City Fathers, although all theatres could be closed at any time if the plays were seen as politically subversive. Towards the end of his career, William Shakespeare not only worked at the Blackfriars, but he also bought the Gate-House to the monastery. As far as we know he never lived there, choosing to rent it out, but there was much talk at the time of ancient tunnels leading from here to beneath the old monastery. Also the scenes in the book set in the vaults are based in the fact that the King's Men leased this area, whilst owning the grand hall where the Playhouse was housed.

Most theatres were open to the elements and could only be used in the summer, but the enclosed Blackfriars offered new possibilities for creative expression, enhancing the theatrical atmosphere. Special effects were used in *The Tempest* such as props lowered from The Heavens, a box suspended from the ceiling, and it is likely that Shakespeare wrote the play with its presentation as an indoor production in mind. The young Miranda, in this imaginary story, witnessed some of the mysteries of Shakespeare and the King's Men as they rehearsed *The Tempest*. It is intriguing to think what insights and wonders the audience of 1611 experienced as this magical tale of an Enchanted Island was enacted before them at the Blackfriars, lit from above by flickering lamps hanging from the ceiling.

There are no surviving pictures of the Playhouse in 1611. Images in this book are based on an original impression by J.H. Farrar, of a drawing appearing in the book *Shakespeare's Blackfriars Playhouse* by Irwin Smith (New York University, 1964). The theatre hall was probably some 15 metres wide and 22 metres long with a gallery on three sides and a stage on the fourth. Unlike the Globe, there was no standing room and the pit was filled with benches. Music was a great feature at the theatre. Musicians entertained the audience whilst the candles were trimmed between acts, and it may also have been the first playhouse in London to use scenery and sound effects extensively.

As the name implies, the King's Men theatre troupe was granted its licence to perform by King James I and was the most important group of actors of the period. William Shakespeare was both an actor with the company, a shareholder and the principal playwright. He was also a partner in the ownership of the Blackfriars and Globe theatres. It is likely that the Blackfriars was the focus for the last five years of Shakespeare's playwriting. The home he bought within walking distance of the theatre, known as the

Blackfriars Gate-House, was left in his will to his daughter Susannah.

The Blackfriars Playhouse continued until the Puritans were finally granted the right to enforce the closure of the London theatres in 1642. The grand meeting hall, housing the Playhouse, was eventually demolished in 1655, marking the end of an era.

Where is The Blackfriars Playhouse in the City of London today?

With no plaque and nothing unusual to draw the attention of passersby, the name Playhouse Yard is the only clue to the historical background of this area. Yet it is one of few remaining places that can boast genuine links with England's greatest dramatist. The author is in the process of generating support for a statue or some permanent reminder of the Playhouse and William Shakespeare in Playhouse Yard.

Close to the Blackfriars public house, Playhouse Yard leads to a hidden churchyard and a maze of alleys. These would have been familiar to Miranda and William Shakespeare when he lived and worked here at the end of the 16th century and up to 1613.

The Blackfriars was big enough to hold between 600 and 700 people and Burbage's company, first called the Lord Chamberlain's Men and then the King's Men, would have performed many of the plays that Shakespeare had written here and at their sister Playhouse, the Globe on Bankside. The works of other writers were also presented; amongst them Ben Johnson's *Every Man in his Humour* in which Shakespeare performed as an actor in 1598.

Francis Bacon, Ciphers and the Elizabethan Alphabet

Sir Francis Bacon was an eminent philosopher, secret service agent for Queen Elizabeth, possible leader of the Rosicrucians and writer of important books such as the *Meditationes Sacrae* (1597), *The Advancement of Learning* (1605), *In Felicem Memoriam Elizabethae*, a eulogy for Queen Elizabeth 1 written in 1609 and *New Atlantis* published in 1627. The new *King James Bible* completed in English by forty-seven scholars and published in 1611 was overseen by Bacon on behalf of the King for all people in the land to read and use in the new Church of England. Bacon was also a secret supporter of the arts and theatre which he saw as an important vehicle for the development and expansion of the English language.

Sir Francis Bacon learnt the use of ciphers whilst in the secret service and the simplest of the ciphers used by him and his colleagues were numerical ones, wherein each letter of the alphabet has an equivalent numerical value. The basic Simple Ciphers are: A = 1, B = 2, through to Z = 24 or using the root numbers 1 to 9, A = 1, K= 1, and so forth. When ciphering words from this period it is important to remember that the Elizabethan alphabet had 24 letters compared with our present day 26.

Simple Cipher
(based on the Elizabethan Alphabet of 24 letters)

A	B	C	D	E	F	G	H	I/J	K	L	M
1	2	3	4	5	6	7	8	9	10/1	11/2	12/3

N	O	P	Q	R	S	T	U/V	W	X	Y	Z
13/4	14/5	15/6	16/7	17/8	18/9	19/1	20/2	21/3	22/4	23/5	24/6

Using the above table, the ciphers shown in this book can be worked out as follows:

BACON = 33 (known to be his cipher signature number)

FREE = 33 ('Free' was the original meaning of 'Francis')

In this story two sections from *The Tempest* have been
quoted, which allude to Bacon's identity:

In Act I Scene 2 Miranda speaks to her father Prospero:
You have often
<u>B</u>egun to tell me what I am, but stopped
<u>A</u>nd left me to a bootless inquisition,
<u>Con</u>cluding, 'Stay, not yet'.

The final word in the First Folio edition of *The Tempest*
(spoken by Prospero) is FREE (Act V, Scene I):
As you from crimes would pardoned be,
*Let your indulgence set me **free**.*

T.T. (The title of the play *The Tempest*) is possibly
another way of showing thirty-three and it is interesting
that in the *First Part of King Henry the Fourth*, the name
'Francis' appears thirty-three times in one sequence of
Act II Scene IV. To attain this end, obviously awkward
sentences were required, such as: *Anon, Francis? No,*
Francis, but tomorrow, Francis; or, Francis, a-Thursday;
or indeed, Francis, when thou wilt. But Francis!

For those interested in further research there is also
a reverse cipher that was used at the time.

Reverse Cipher
(based on the Elizabethan Alphabet of 24 letters)

A	B	C	D	E	F	G	H	I/J	K	L	M
24/6	23/5	22/4	21/3	20/2	19/1	18/9	17/8	16/7	15/6	14/5	13/4

N	O	P	Q	R	S	T	U/V	W	X	Y	Z
12/3	11/2	10/1	9	8	7	6	5	4	3	2	1

The reverse count of the word FREE is 67 and the simple count of the word FRANCIS is also 67, which further adds weight to the way ciphers were possibly hidden in the play *The Tempest*.

There is compelling evidence that even the memorial statue to William Shakespeare in Westminster Abbey contains a cipher which shows that its designers were well aware of the involvement by Francis Bacon in the playwright's work. Please see the book by K. F Hollenbach in the Bibliography.

Numerology and the significance of the number Thirty-Three

In the time of Shakespeare, the nature and the meaning of numbers, symbols and heraldry held rich significance for playwrights, writers and scholars. Numbers, in particular, were believed to provide the secret key to the deepest mysteries of God and man. As an example, Queen Elizabeth I's astrologer Dr. John Dee stated in one of his translations that 'by numbers, a way is had, to the searching out, and understanding of everything, able to be known.' The Greek philosopher Pythagoras said 'the world is built upon the power of numbers'.

In our story the number thirty-three is shown to be the personal cipher of Sir Francis Bacon. Three and thirty-three are both recognised as special symbolic numbers throughout Rosicrucian and Freemasonry teachings and appear to have had special significance in the Elizabethan and Jacobean era. For instance, history books available in Shakespeare's time describe that during the assassination of Julius Caesar twenty-three wounds were inflicted by his attackers; however Shakespeare increased these to thirty-three for no apparent reason. (Octavius refers to 'three and thirty wounds' in the play *Julius Caesar* Act V, Scene I).

Three has been known for centuries as representing spiritual growth in symbols such as the triangle and the fleur-de-lis and nearly every religion has three gods as the principal deities: Brahma, Vishnu and Shiva represent a triad for Hindus, and God the Father, God the Son and God the Holy Spirit, for Christians. The number thirty-three is equally important and is found over and over again in references within Christianity, Judaism, Hindu and Tibetan religions. When corresponding to an individual's name thirty-three is said to prognosticate that the individual is a highly-developed person spiritually or has such an intention. As this was Sir Francis Bacon's personal cipher this may be a further indication of his position as spiritual head of the Rosicrucians in Elizabethan times. Each of the numbers 1 to 9 have meaning attached to them, and for those interested there are many books explaining the significance of numbers, which is known generically as numerology, and you can refer to some of the books shown in the reading list at the end of this section for more information.

The Apothecary

Miranda's meetings with Shakespeare is set mainly at an apothecary and unbeknown to the author when writing the original Miranda story, there is today a lane called Apothecary Street, close to Playhouse Yard, London EC4 (the site of the original Playhouse). It is intriguing to think that an apothecary may have existed there, as described in this book.

The Mummer

A *Mummer* (from 'momer' to mime, and 'momon' a mask) was originally one of a group of masked performers in a play. As with most arts there are three levels of interpretation and it is the first that refers to the mixture of pantomime, Morris dancing and mime primarily associated with the word. In the writer's opinion, the second level is best characterised by the advanced skill known as 'method acting', used by eminent actors such as Al Pacino and Robert de Niro. In *Miranda's meetings with Shakespeare* the word *mummer* is used to describe a little known third level, which is the bringing to life of *imprinted history*, the lives of Kings and Queens, and other events held in the collective consciousness of a nation or community. Other examples of this kind include the Noh players of Japan, and aboriginal native dance and music.

Boy Actors and Women on Stage in 1611

Boy actors, such as Nathan in our story, were

apprentices to troupes such as the King's Men. The up-and-coming young actors were a source of new acting talent for the adult companies. Also, the Blackfriars Playhouse was used by boy troupes and boys' companies throughout the period. It is interesting that the term *playboy* has today lost its original meaning as a boy who played female roles in the plays.

There was no law at the time preventing women from acting upon the public stage. It was, however, an accepted social convention that only boys or men acted in public. Women could act in private masques and there are even occasional references to women acting on stage in the Elizabethan and Jacobean period. But it was only after the Civil War and the Restoration, when Charles II granted licenses for theatre troupes to operate in London once again, that these included women actors. As Miranda lived to an old age it is conceivable that she could have seen her granddaughter act legitimately on the stage at venues like the Little Theatre in Haymarket after 1660.

Ghosts and Apparitions

There are many references in books available to read at the British Library to ghosts or apparitions being seen in the playhouses or on stage during the Elizabethan and Jacobean period, and theatres today still maintain the tradition of keeping a light on stage overnight to ward off ghosts. It is possible that the environment in the City, without cars, mobile phones, electrical machinery and so on, allowed paranormal activity to be witnessed more easily. In his role as an actor, whilst playing Hamlet's ghost at the Playhouse, Shakespeare is said to have witnessed a phantom that materialized from within the great wall of the old City.

There is much to suppose that actors at the time experienced what we might call the *mystical*, whilst on stage. There is also some evidence that acting troupes, such as the King's Men, could summon the presence of great people and events from the past through acting skill, barding and their plays.

Bryan Ritz, 2012

References for Further Reading

Armin R. — *Frown Strong – A Conversation with Merlin*, Cobwebs Press, 1975

Barnham M. — *The Cambridge Guide to Theatre*, Cambridge, 1995

Brown I. — *Shakespeare*, The Reprint Society, 1951

Brown I. — *Shakespeare and His World*, Lutterworth, 1964

Bryson B. — *Shakespeare*, Harper, 2007

Byrne R. — *The Secret*, Simon & Schuster, 2006

Chambers E.K. — *Chambers Elizabethan Stage*, Oxford, 1923

Cook J. — *Women in Shakespeare*, Harrap, 1980

Cook J. — *Shakespeare's Players*, Harrap, 1983

Gordon E.O. — *Prehistoric London*, Artisan, 1914

Gurdjieff G.I. — *Life Is Real Only Then, When I Am*, Compass, 1974

Hall Manly P. — *The Secret Teachings of All Ages*, Privately Published 1928

Hall, Sir P. — *Exposed by the Mask*, Oberon, 2000

Holderness, Prof. G.   *The Prince of Denmark*, University of Hertfordshire, 2002

Hartnell P. (Editor)   *The Oxford Companion to the Theatre*, Oxford, 1983

Holden A.   *William Shakespeare – His Life and Work*, Little Brown, 1999

Hollenbach K. F   *Francis Rosicross*, Dunsinane Hill Publications, 1996

Kermode F.   *Shakespeare's Language*, Allen Lane, 2000

Nuttall A.   *Shakespeare the Thinker*, Yale, 2007

Ouspensky P.D.   *In Search of the Miraculous,* Routledge, 1931

Shapiro J.   *1599 – A Year in the Life of William Shakespeare*, Faber, 2005

Smith I.   *Shakespeare's Blackfriars Playhouse*, New York University, 1964